HYENA

HYENA

JUDE ANGELINI

G
GALLERY BOOKS
New York   London   Toronto   Sydney   New Delhi

G

Gallery Books
A Division of Simon & Schuster, Inc.
1230 Avenue of the Americas
New York, NY 10020

Edited by Andrea Grano, Jeremie Ruby-Strauss, and Alison Callahan
Illustrations by Frank Ryan

First Gallery Books trade paperback edition September 2014

GALLERY BOOKS and colophon are registered trademarks
of Simon & Schuster, Inc.

For information about special discounts for bulk purchases,
please contact Simon & Schuster Special Sales at 1-866-506-1949
or business@simonandschuster.com.

The Simon & Schuster Speakers Bureau can bring authors to your live event. For
more information or to book an event contact the Simon & Schuster Speakers
Bureau at 1-866-248-3049 or visit our website at www.simonspeakers.com.

Interior design by Davina Mock-Maniscalco

Manufactured in the United States of America

10   9   8   7   6   5

Library of Congress Cataloging-in-Publication Data is available.

ISBN 978-1-4767-8930-9
ISBN 978-1-4767-8931-6 (ebook)

For Julie. I figured it out too late. For my daughter, Assia.
For my friends and family who raised me.

contents

HYENA

top gun

I'M IN A CAB LEANING MY face out the window, gone off Percocets and ketamine. This motherfucker crosses the street in front of me looking just like Goose from *Top Gun*. I'm thinking that was fucked-up how he died, leaving a wife and kid.

I say, "Rest in peace, Goose." And the cab drives off.

Earlier at Jeff's high-rise apartment, I copped some drugs from a Dominican with a silver briefcase. Jeff got the MDMA, I got the vials of Ketamine. I cooked the K in the oven. He had some Australian chick licking the Molly off his fingertips. Just the three of us. They're rolling, I'm not.

She said she doesn't do K cuz it makes her lose control.

I tell her in that case, do as much as you want.

She does as much as she wants; Jeff does, too. We're chopping it up with his cheese knife, snorting the lines with a wrinkly one-dollar bill; it's all the Dominican left us. This goes on for hours, rolling and K-holes and she's grinding her teeth, rubbing her thighs together. I tell her to come cuddle, but it's awkward. She don't even know me. She gets up and we pretend like it never happened.

It's around then I realize, she's not fucking me solo. Either he's gonna fuck or we're all gonna fuck. So how bad do you want it? Bad enough to see your homeboy naked, hairy ass and all? I smashed chicks back in the day with cats that are like my brothers. Toss 'em up, one in the mouth, one in the vagina, it's nothing. But I don't know with Jeff.

Shit, if we can be all the way honest, it's kind of what I prefer for threesomes—two dudes and a chick. With two dudes, I can focus on the chick. With two girls it gets complicated; I don't know where to look, who to pay attention to. I'm trying to eat pussy and smash at the same time. Shit's hard, like doing algebra.

I tried it once with Annie and her homegirl after a night of whiskey and muscle relaxers. I couldn't get my dick to stay hard. I even ate two Viagras, nothing. I just ended up eating them out and we're hitting each other.

She'd be like, "Eat my pussy, bitch," and slap me upside the head.

And I'd be like, "Yeah, take that, bitch," and smack her across the face.

I usually don't go for all that bitch shit, but since I couldn't get my dick hard I figured we were on some aggro dyke shit, so I let it slide. When they came, they excused themselves and went home with no eye contact. I'm standing there buck naked, limp dick, thinking about how we just murdered my roommate's new couch.

That was the last threesome I had. I don't know if I wanna jump back in with hairy Jeff and the assless Australian, banging it out doggy-style while he's getting head, shooting me a thumbs-up. I feel like he'd wink at me midstroke, like, "Yeah, we're killing this, bro!" and I wouldn't know where to look so I'd look down at his nipples and a piece of me would die inside.

So I bail and Jeff fucks and I'm in the cab thinking about Goose. We would've had to have been best friends like Maverick and Goose to run a busto on that chick, or she would've had to look like Nicole Kidman to get me to double up with him. But she's not that cute and we're not that close and that's okay. I'm nodding my head to Modest Mouse on my iPod looking at the East River as the cabbie drives over the Williamsburg Bridge. I kinda wanna tell him to turn around. But I don't.

So I link up with Brad and we rage all night just like the last six nights. Popping pills and doing K. We're on his roof watching the sunrise and talking about aliens. New York looks like a Nintendo game, like Megaman. Shit gets real digital on this ketamine.

"This place ain't natural," I say. "We been around for thousands and thousands of years on this planet, and now they got us walking on concrete. What the fuck is that? Shit, I couldn't tell you the last time I walked barefoot on some earth, touched some dirt. Shit out here, you gotta take a fucking train just to lay on some grass. They trying to kill us out here."

New York is nice to look at, but I'm ready to go.

We're back down on the fire escape taking rails of K to the face. I'm swabbing the blood out of my nose with wet Q-tips, giving him the ketamine pep talk to get him motivated. He's like a bunch of my friends: creative and talented and not doing shit.

He's scared. I recognize it, cuz I'm scared, too. Doing shit is scary, waking up is scary, getting up every morning, looking in the mirror, and trying to like yourself is fucking hard. I get it. I keep telling him, "All you got to do is do!" I'm saying it over and over. "All you got to do is do!"

I'm hugging him, telling him I love him.

I woulda ran a busto with Brad.

It's six thirty in the morning. I go to bed. I got a flight this afternoon.

I call Assia from the airport. It's her birthday. My old boss Tony from the pager store told me that no matter what, you always gotta see your kid on her birthday. When old people tell you shit, you should listen. I kept that up till her grandparents moved her down to Florida. Now I give her phone calls.

I call Assia, but she doesn't answer. I leave her a message on her birthday. My daughter gets a message. I tell her I love her. I tell her I'm proud of her. I tell her fifteen years ago on this day when they pulled her out of her mom, her head was all pointy and I was pissed-off with the doctor that they messed up her head. I tell her they told me it's just from the birth canal and that her head would be okay. I tell her her head turned out just fine and I couldn't be happier with her. I tell her I love her, I tell her goodbye.

I get on my plane and fly.

shower me with your love

I GOT HER IN THE STUDIO, little punk rock, porn chick. She had the sunglasses on, dark hair with the bangs, tats and all that. Stood about four foot somethin'.

I say, "Look at you. You adorable little young thing, get in my pocket." She's laughing.

We're on the air talking about all the nasty things she's done: fucking and sucking and all the run-of-the-mill shit. Then she starts talking about pissing. Pissing in cups, pissing on dudes, dudes pissing on her. The whole nine.

I tell her, "That's hot."

She's like, "Yeah it is."

I'm talking shit. "Bet you won't piss on me."

She calls my bluff. "I'll piss on you."

We go to music.

How we gonna do this? Do I lay down and have her do it on my chest? I look at the carpet; it's filthy. I tell her to do it on my leg.

I'm outside the studio, looking for a garbage bag to catch the piss.

"Tully, where the trash bags at?"

He gives me a look, tells me where to go.

We're back in the studio; the song's done. I'm in the chair, garbage bag down, pants rolled up. She straddles my leg, pulls her skirt up, and pushes her panties to the side.

Surprisingly, my dick's hard as hell. This shit's kinda sexy to me. I guess I'm the kind of guy that likes to get pissed on. Like a toilet.

I'm a toilet.

I put the mike to her crotch.

She goes. A long, hot, steady stream of piss hits my leg, runs down my ankle, down my foot, to my toes and onto the bag. It's making a pool.

"I shoulda gave you a forty!"

"Yeah, right?!"

I wipe up with a paper towel; we take phone calls. Cats are saying I'm crazy. Crazy like a fox. They're calling me a bitch for letting her piss on my leg. Call me what you want, but you're calling.

Show's over.

I'm like, "We should do ecstasy and fuck. You wanna do ecstasy and fuck?"

She smiles, "Yeah."

Can't do it at her house; she lives three deep in a one-bed-room apartment. We end up at my house. I feed her some E and take some myself. We're making out in the bed. My heart's racing, I get flush, the E's kicking in.

She wants to fuck.

I'm doing it all slow and sensual, ecstasy style. Taking my time, like I'm doing something, making love and shit.

She wants it harder, so I do it harder. Now she wants it harder than that. So I'm fuckin' her harder than that. She wants it harder still.

These porn chicks and their hard fucking. They come into the studio and we gotta give 'em vibrators that hit like jackhammers cuz their clits are so blew out.

I'm three minutes into fucking this chick and I'm already sweating. I'm sposed to do this for another three hours? I'm holding her little baby legs in each hand by the ankles, smashing till my dick is numb. This is some bullshit.

My dick goes soft in five minutes. I blame the E.

"Hey babe, it's the E. The shit made me go soft. I'ma take a Viagra."

"You sure you okay?"

I'm burning up sweating, heart jumping out of my chest, pill popping trying to fuck a porn star like a porn star. "Yeah."

I take a Viagra. We hit the living room; she wants to hear Lil Wayne.

We're laid out on the shag carpet, I'm going down on her, rolling our asses off. It's euphoric. I'm feeling warm all over. There's no place on earth I'd rather be right now, than in between her legs. Then it hits me—Lil Wayne is so fucking good!

She cums.

I feel the heat between my legs; the Viagra's kicking in. I get on top, we fuck for a while on the floor. Take a break. I love drugs. This is the best. We're talking about life and shit like that. You know. Really vibing.

She gets up to pee.

I'm watching her little naked body as she runs down the hall.

Something's off.

Her gait's not really a gait. It's more like a waddle. And her torso's longer than I remember, her limbs are shorter than I recall, and her head's big as hell for her body.

She scampers like a midget. But she's too tall to be a midget.

Hell naw!

I'm fucking a dwarf, a tall-ass dwarf. Shit's got me fucked-up.

I had a midget on my bucket list, but that was just talk.

Now I finally got one, and I don't know what to do with it. I always thought I'd be prepared for this, but I got hit out of nowhere with a surprise dwarf while rolling my balls off.

I'm sitting there buck naked on the carpet, eyeballs twitching, teeth grinding, and I'm getting all emotional. Thinking, Goddamn, you're doing ecstasy with midgets. This is fucking crazy, man. What are you gonna do? Don't say nothing to her, you don't wanna hurt her feelings. It's not her fault she's a dwarf. She's just playing the hand she was dealt.

Then I start thinking about people doing the best they can with what they got, motherfuckers running marathons on prosthetic legs, the little old man at the bus stop with threadbare clothes but he's clean and they're tucked in and I damn near well up.

Life is beautiful.

The toilet flushes.

She waddles back into the room, kisses me on the mouth, *and lays down next to me real dwarflike.*

Ain't shit to do but finish what we started. I pop another pill and give her one, too. We fuck until my dick doesn't work, so I pop another Viagra and fuck her some more. Hard as I can.

epiphany

WE DIDN'T HAVE JEWS IN MY neighborhood growing up. I didn't think about them one way or another. My auntie was the housekeeper for some; I never met 'em. We weren't allowed in the house, but they'd give us hand-me-downs and that was pretty cool.

When I came to LA, I used to cuss out the Hasidic ones. These motherfuckers would jaywalk a caravan of strollers across the street right in front of the car and not have the decency to even look up.

They'd do that shit to me and I'd holler out the window, "You're welcome, bitch!"

And they'd still ignore me.

My best friend Andrea's ex-husband was Jewish, so she was always riding for Israel and shit. She'd be in the passenger seat ducking down, shushing me.

"Jude!"

"What?"

"You sound anti-Semitic."

"I'm not anti-Semitic, I fucked tons of Jewish chicks."

"Jude, you'll fuck anything with a hole. That doesn't count."

And I'd be like, "They're jaywalking all up in front of the car like they own the place and don't even fucking wave."

Then she'd say, "Black people do that, and you don't get mad at them."

"Well yeah, they walk slow as hell, but that's cuz they got an inferiority complex. They think by having me wait at the light that's gonna make up for the sixties. And at least they acknowledge you. They'll stare you down. These Jewish cats pretend you don't even exist! Fuck that! Lose your little I'm-better-than-you God-chose-me attitude you Jewish motherfuckers!"

She'd just shake her head and say, "Anti-Semite."

We'd go round and round about it all the way to Bed Bath & Beyond.

But that's all I thought about the Jews. That I liked fucking the chicks, the Hasidic ones were assholes, and whatever I learned from the Anne Frank movie.

When I got to New York and got the job at Sirius, I was at some club with a few of the bosses and a couple of 'em come over to me. One of 'em puts his arm around me, all chummy with this shit-eating grin, and he says under his breath, "Welcome, welcome. It's good to see we got another member of the Tribe here."

I say, "What?"

So he says it louder with a nod: "It's good to have another member of the Tribe here."

I'm confused. I don't know what the fuck he's talking about.

I say, "Member of the Tribe? What tribe you talkin' bout?"

He goes, "The Jewish tribe; you're the Rude Jew, aren't you?"

I say, "Nah I'm Rude Jude, J-U-D-E. My folks were Catholic, my dad's Italian. I'm not Jewish."

And he doesn't say anything; he just takes his arm from around my shoulder and they all disperse.

They ain't say shit else to me for the rest of the day.

Who the fuck does that? I don't run up on Italians with some secret handshake.

I got it into my head that there was some secret Jewish club going on. As the weeks went by I noticed that damn near all my bosses were Jewish. Yom Kippur, there'd be fucking tumbleweeds rolling through upper management's office cuz nobody was there. The percentages don't add up. How the fuck does a group of motherfuckers who represent 2 percent of the population in America represent 90 percent of my bosses? Jewish nepotism.

I'm looking at these cats bitter as hell, like, "How you get this job?" This goes on for years. I'm busting my ass, watching our stock prices fall, and these cats keep their jobs. I'm looking at dudes collecting paychecks and I don't even know what the fuck they do and I'm mad. I get this anger in me, this resentment.

One night, I'm out with these motherfuckers and some other manager cats and they're all Jewish and doing business with each other with their nice watches. Fuck these dudes. I like 'em, but I don't respect what the fuck they do and I'm jealous that they're doing better than me. I leave.

At the crib, I'm trying to unwind. It's one in the morning. I got work the next day but I'm like, "Fuck it, I'ma do some Whip-Its."

I got a box of nitrous cartridges, a cracker, and a punchy balloon. I'm doing four Whip-Its at a time. I'm sucking it down, passing out, coming to. I decide I'm gonna jerk off and catch a nut while the wah-wah-wahs are going on in my head. I'm out of lotion, I get the olive oil, I got my pants around my ankles, I'm looking at Internet porn, trying to find the perfect scene, trying to time it just right.

I find one. She's got a fat ass, she's blowing him. I'm staring at her ass, watching her head bob up and down. I hit the balloon, the wah-wah-wahs come, I'm jerkin', I bust.

That was the shit.

I'm leaning back in my chair. Pants down, dress shirt on, I got a shriveled balloon in my left hand, semen's on my right. Enjoy the moment. I barely soak it in, look to my left, and there's four more Whip-Its in the box. Let's go. I kick off my pants, wipe myself down with my boxers, throw on some music, and get to filling that balloon.

I start hitting it, Smashing Pumpkins is on; "1979," that's my shit. I'm breathing in 'n' out on the balloon, in and out. I sound like Darth Vader. I'm thinking about my bosses and how they're all richer than me and how come? Do they deserve it? I'm thinking about the Jew Club of insiders and how they look out for each other and I'm like, Fuck them dudes. And the wah-wah-wahs are coming but I still just keep breathing it in and my head goes fuzzy and I'm dreaming and I'm playing out scenarios from the day in my head for what feels like hours and I keep sucking in that gas and there's a thud.

I come to. I hear Billy Corgan singing, "Weeee don't even care, as restless as we are. . . ."

I'm facedown on my JCPenney shag carpet and it hits me. I bet them Jewish motherfuckers aren't facedown in the carpet, naked from the waist down, dick covered with olive oil, passed out from nitrous on a school night. My mouth tastes like metal, my stomach's rotten. I get up, go to the bathroom, and puke.

squeaky clean

I WAS DRIVING WITH MY DAD in his Chevette when he decided to have the sex talk with me. On the way to my mom's, we just drove past Old Perch Road when he turns down the radio, looks over at me, and says all solemn, "Jude."

I'm thinking I'm in trouble for something. I look at him back, I say, "Yeah?"

"Do you know what cunnilingus is?"

I didn't want to have a sex talk. I already knew about sex from health class and from stealing dirty magazines from Merle, our downstairs neighbor. He was on welfare; he'd lie in his bed all day smoking weed and reading sci-fi novels. He had a long stick he used to change the channels from his bed. He'd poke at the TV with it when he wanted to see something different.

When he'd run up to the gas station for smokes, I'd walk into his apartment and steal the *Playboys* and *Hustlers* and take 'em back upstairs to beat off.

I knew where the dick went, how babies were made. I was fourteen. This wasn't the fifties when motherfuckers believed in storks.

My dad's doing this shit he does with his face when he tries to look sincere, this half frown with puppy-dog eyes.

"Jude. Do you know what cunnilingus is?"

"Naw, what's cunnilingus?"

He says, "When a man loves a woman very much, he takes her into the bedroom and puts his mouth on her vagina, and he licks it with his tongue."

I look at him disgusted. "Eating pussy? Hell naw! I'm not putting my face where some fucking bitch bleeds out of once a month! That's fucking gross."

At the time I really felt like this. I had never even touched a pussy, so the idea of eating one seemed daunting. Plus, I grew up with black kids and eating pussy was some bitch shit.

My dad keeps pressing, "No, Jude, listen to me. The ladies love when you go down on them. You lick their clitoris till they go fucking crazy and cum." And he sticks out his tongue and he touches his nose. "See?" He used to do that a lot.

I tell him, "I don't care what the fuck they do, I ain't eating no pussy."

He says, "You will."

I say, "I won't."

He says, "Oh you're gonna eat pussy. You're gonna lick it clean."

"Look, Pop, I'm not eatin' no motherfuckin' pussy—chill out with that shit!"

And he stares at me and I'm glaring back and he turns his head. We drive in silence for a while and I'm grateful.

It was tight quarters in the Chevette. My shoulder touched his shoulder and both our shoulders touched the window. My pop's a big-ass Italian from Leominster, Massachusetts. He says "cah" instead of "car" and "bah" instead of "bar" and he claims he knows people in the Mob. He was always telling stories about Porky Valeri getting his hand smashed to bits with a ball-peen hammer and how his buddies took some Puerto Rican into the mountains, shoved a funnel in his ass, poured battery acid in it, and then threw him down the hill.

He was always talking about how he coulda been in the Mob but he decided to go straight. So that's why we're having this sex talk wedged into his rusted-out, piece-of-shit Chevette. Taking me from his shitty one-bedroom apartment where we lived to another piece-of-shit apartment, where I lived with my mom, because he decided to go straight.

"Jude."

"What, man?"

"Do you know what anilingus is?"

"Don't even tell me."

"That's when if you love a woman very, very much, like how I loved ya motha, you take her in the bathroom, wash her up real good, and get her squeaky clean. Then you lay her down on the bed on her stomach and you lick her asshole. You spread her cheeks and you tongue her asshole. I used to do it to your motha all the time, she couldn't get enough of it, it'd drive her nuts. Make sure you get her nice and squeaky clean, though; you don't wanna get shit in your mouth because the fecal matter'll make you sick. That's what the Vietcong did in 'Nam: they dipped spikes in shit and buried them in pits and set up booby traps to kill soldiers. They'd get these puncture wounds with shit in 'em and it'd fester. . . ."

I sat there in silence staring at the trees out the window while he went on about 'Nam and eating my mom's ass. He was always talking about fucking my mom. Poor guy, never did get over losing her.

my morning

I'VE HIT A NEW LOW. I got my phone in one hand, my dick in the other. I'm in bed jerking off to chicks drinking urine. Regular porn doesn't cut it anymore. It'll only get worse. It might be an elephant dick tomorrow. Let me just take care of this fucking thing, beat it to submission, then I can face the day.

It's better than jerking off to old sex with my ex-girlfriend. That's no way to start the morning, with some brokenhearted shame nut.

Then I'm thinking about her all day, thinking it's Julie every time I see a brunette from a distance with full hips. Waiting for her to turn around, walking faster to see her face, follow her for a block or two, just to talk to her, what are you gonna say? Nothing. Wrong person. Never mind.

I wonder if she sees ghosts, too.

I rub the cum on my belly and wait for it to dry before I throw the covers back on. The phone's on my side with the movie still playing, this chick lapping up piss out of the bowl.

used and abused

I WAS LOOKING TO MEET A chick who played backgammon in my area, so I posted an ad for it on Craigslist. I kept it straightforward yet vague. That way if she was cute, I could try and fuck her, and if she was ugly, we'd just play the game and I could try and fuck her friends.

It read something like this:

Backgammon Anyone?

do you love playing backgammon? me too! Looking for new people to play backgammon with. i hope to start a club. please contact me if you're interested. i'm located in the Hollywood area.

I might as well have written, "Hi I'm Jude, I'm on suicide watch, sometimes I wake up crying."

I genuinely love the game; it's poetic, it mirrors life. You can do everything right, but you get one wrong roll and lose in the end. But over time the better player will come out on top if you just keep playing. When I put out the ad, I thought that women might find this hobby quirky and charming. They don't. It's about as quirky and charming to chicks as a captain's hat and a corncob pipe.

One person answered. She was from Alaska with an extremely high voice. She called and said, "Hi, I'm from Alaska. My voice is high."

We set up something for later that week. I show up at Starbucks to play backgammon with her. She rolls up riding a Rascal scooter. Turned out she was retarded. I beat her twice and left.

I went back on Craigslist. I thought maybe I should check out the Casual Encounters page, since the backgammon didn't work out. I came across an ad from a woman looking to have rough casual sex on a biweekly basis. This might be fun. I've choked out chicks and smacked women around in the sack before, so I figured I could hack it.

I hit her up. She hit me back. We send pictures. In her photo she had on a camouflage army hat and rave gear circa 1999. Her face was average; she had large tits. I've fucked uglier chicks.

We arranged to meet at some dive bar in Pasadena.

I was at the bar drinking pineapple juice when she walked in. The picture she sent was from 1999. What entered was a 2010 plain-faced, overweight, matronly woman, in business slacks and a blouse. She looked like she managed an office somewhere. She pulled up to the bar. The dude next to me looked at her, then looked at me, and laughed. I pretended like I didn't see him.

We talked awhile; she told me she managed an office somewhere. She lived in the same apartment with her husband and boyfriend and that both men knew she was here meeting me and that we were supposed to fuck. She told me she had rape fantasies and a high IQ. She struck me as a woman who played Magic: The Gathering.

The conversation was cool but I wasn't really attracted to her. I stayed for two drinks and excused myself to leave. She followed me to my car. I went to hug her goodbye; she rubbed my dick through my jeans and said, "So, you wanna take this to the next level?"

"What level is that?"

"We go back to your place and fuck."

I'm hesitant. I say, "I don't know. It's late, I'm tired. I'm not really up for raping you tonight. Maybe another time, like next week or something."

She squeezes my dick. "You don't have to rape me, we can just have regular sex."

My shit's getting hard. I look at her. "No rape, just a quickie?"

She says, "Just a quickie."

She sure is persistent. What if this is a setup? What if her boyfriend and husband are in another car and they're gonna follow me to the crib and they're gonna rob me? Rob my house while I'm fucking this broad. Knock me out and steal my kidney. But I do like the way she's rubbing my dick through the jeans and she does have some big-ass titties and she ain't that ugly out here where it's dark.

"What the hell, follow me."

I take her the roundabout way, zigzagging through neighborhoods just in case we're being followed, checking the rearview for extra headlights.

We get back to the crib, I got her on the couch. I got the lights turned down. I start kissing on her and she starts whimpering, "No no . . . don't. No."

I'm moving too fast, so I stop. She grabs me and starts kissing me again. A minute into it she starts with her "No, no, nos." So I stop.

"Are you okay?"

"Yeah, I'm okay."

"You keep like, crying and shit."

"I'm just nervous."

We start up again and she's whimpering. This stop-go shit goes on for like five minutes and I'm kind of freaking out. I'm not really into teary orgasms, unless that's what we're going for.

But this is reminding me of when I was a teenager and I thought I was gonna catch a rape case. I pulled this black chick. She was fucking with some lame, born-again Christian but I got her to stay the night with me anyway. We're messing around, making out, I ended up eating her out, cuz I'm white and that's what we do. She's gripping my head, she gets off. I'm at the edge of the bed wiping up and she's like, "What just happened?!"

I say, "What do you mean what just happened?"

She says, "I woke up and I'm all wet on my legs—what did you do? Why are my panties off?!"

Woke up? We was just making out. When'd she fall asleep?

I look at this evil bitch; she's fucking crazy. She knows damn well what we did and why her panties are off. She's trying to act like I mouth-raped her.

That's how you wanna play it? Fine.

I say, "You must've kicked your panties off in your sleep, because we didn't do nothing."

"Are you sure?"

I'm sitting there with all types of pussy on my face—my shit's glistening like a glazed doughnut.

"I swear to God we didn't do nothing. I pinky promise."

And I spooned her ass to sleep.

This bitch felt bad about cheating on her man, so she was threatening some sexual assault shit to keep me quiet. After that, I made sure I got verbal consent from any chick I ever messed with before we did anything.

The Christian college girl hit me up on MySpace a couple years back. She's in Vegas, a dancer now. She was wearing a bikini holding a broadsword in her profile pic. She wanted to link up again. I never hit her back.

So now I'm a little weirded out by the Craigslist lady telling me to stop every two seconds, fake crying and shit. I'm not really trying to deal with rape unless we agree on it and last time I checked, I told this chick I wasn't raping her.

She's sitting there whimpering on the couch. I say, "What

are you doing? I thought we were sposed to just fuck. Am I hurting you? Why are you crying? Maybe you should just go."

I put my hand on her stomach, trying to be sweet, and it's real hard and it's poking out. I say, "What's that?"

She lifts up her shirt; she's wearing a girdle, but her stomach's still protruding. She says, "I'm pregnant."

I say, "How pregnant?"

"Six months."

And I thought she was just fat. There goes my dick, getting hard again.

Sick bastard.

Pregnant pussy's good pussy, cuz it's all swollen like a baboon's ass and extra wet and you can't get her pregnant again. I whisper, "Go to my room."

She does.

We strip, and start fucking. I'm fuckin' her slow and easy like I'm in a Colt 45 commercial; she's not into it at all. I try nice and slow doggie-style, nothing. Get on top. She rides me a minute, maybe. She hops off. We're standing there next to the bed.

She's like, "This isn't working for me. I'm going to need you to rape me."

"What about the baby? I don't wanna hurt the baby."

She says, "You'd have to kick me in the stomach to hurt the baby; don't worry about the baby."

I'm standing there in my bedroom buck naked, condom on my dick, staring at some naked pregnant stranger who wants me to rape her.

I grab her by her neck and slam her onto the bed, hop on top of her, and force myself inside her.

She's screaming, "NoNoNo!!"

One hand's on her throat, choking her; I'm smacking her with the right. "Shut up, bitch!!! Take this fuckin' dick, you dumb whore!"

She makes a feeble attempt to bat at me. I pin her down, put my forearm in her throat, and lean all my weight into her.

She's crying real tears. "No, no please!"

"Shut the fuck up."

I jam my hand into her mouth to gag her. She's gasping and gargling on my fist. She's getting spit all over my hand. I take it out, wipe it on her face, then stuff it back in her mouth.

I tell her I'm gonna rape the shit out of her and send her home to her punk-ass boyfriend and bitch-ass husband when I'm through. This goes on for a while. At one point, I'm palming her face like a basketball, jerking her head all over the bed while she's weakly swatting at me. The whole time I'm trying not to laugh. This shit is ridiculous.

I gotta cum but I don't really know rape-sex etiquette. Do you just fuck real hard till you cum or do you hold off till she cums? I think as a rule, rapists are selfish lovers, but this isn't like official rape.

I go for another five minutes and finally bust, hop up, and say, "Now get up, get dressed, and get the fuck out of my house."

I'm sitting there on the couch, naked, drinking water out of a jelly jar, feeling awesome: like I just raped the shit out of this pregnant bitch. It's not what you do, it's how you do it. I don't care if you're a janitor; just make sure you got the cleanest floors in town.

She comes out. I ask, "How was that?" already knowing the answer: great.

She says, "It was fine."

I say, "What do you mean fine?"

"A little light, but I had fun anyway."

And with that, she walks out the door, gets in her car, and drives back to her men.

collateral damage

WHEN I WAS IN THE SHOWER washing my butt, I felt a lump on my ass. I thought it was a tumor. I thought I was gonna die from ass cancer.

I'm picturing people falling out at my funeral. Wondering how many people'll show. I remind myself to throw out the porn DVDs in the dresser and to clear the hard drive before I die, so my mom won't have to see the shit I jerk off to. I'll go back to Detroit to spend my last days there, maybe smoke some crack. My job'll probably try to hold a memorial for me and fuck it up. By the time I'm out of the shower, I've come to terms with my death.

Went to the doctor that Thursday; turns out it's hemorrhoids. Superbad hemorrhoids. My hemorrhoids got hemorrhoids. And now he's got to cut me.

He explained to me exactly what was going on with my anus, but I really couldn't follow cuz right before his explanation, he raped my asshole with his fingers and cameras and metal rods.

The whole experience made me rethink throwing my finger up a chick's asshole without warning mid-coitus. I probably won't do that anymore.

I used to be reckless with that butt-hole shit. I tried to sodomize every single girl I smashed. Not because it felt great, mind you; it just feels okay. Pussy feels better and there's some downsides to sodomy, like sometimes you end up with shit on your dick.

It's just that if I was gonna fuck, I wanted my dick to hit every hole. So when I saw her months later at the mall with her new man and we were all smiling and nodding and making niceties, I'd be looking at her thinking, "I was up in your butt hole, fuckin'. Great to see you." And then I'd be off to Marshalls to buy Hilfiger shirts on clearance.

I stopped trying to sodomize chicks when I stopped going to the mall for my clothes and chilled out with my anger issues. I mean, if she wants me to fuck her there, sure I will, that's hot, whatever you want, I'm game. Even then, not all the time, cuz if I'm always putting it in her butt, what are we sposed to do on Valentine's Day?

Speaking of sodomy, the doctor shoved all those things up my butt hole and then cut my ass and left me there in a diaper on the gurney. The irony is, these last few weeks, I've been wanting to get my hands on some Vicodin. Well, now I got it. Be careful what you wish for.

I've been on Vicodin these past three days. I keep taking it so I won't shit. I'm afraid to. Vicodin and tighty whities with a maxi-pad shoved in my ass crack, cuz I'm leaking blood.

My mom keeps calling me to see if I'm all right.

I am. I just walk funny and I'm getting used to the tighty whities smashing my balls. I tried to do the maxi-pad with some boxers and that shit fell out in the middle of the road, right next to some kids playing. I tried to kick it across the street, but it kept getting stuck to the pavement, so I just kept walking like it wasn't mine.

Kev took me to the Dodgers game yesterday. The good seats. It was nice to sit out there in the sun, nodding off on opiates while the Cubs whooped the Dodgers' asses. It was fun till some piece-of-shit Dodgers fan started talking shit to us.

We ain't say nothing to this fucking dude and the motherfucker's talking 'bout the "douche-bag Cub fans" in front of him. I'm not even from Chicago. My friends are. I'm waiting for them to say some shit, but they don't. I turn around and it's some day trader sitting with his hot wife and friends.

I tell him to chill out.

He says he was being funny.

I tell him he isn't funny and to stop talking to us.

He starts talking about my accent; his eyes are wild like he's gonna do something, talking to me like he knows karate or some shit.

I'm like, "Bruh, chill out and shut up talking to us."

He's like, "Brah brah brah. What the hell is a brah, brah? Why you talking like that, brah?"

"Cuz I'm from Detroit, bruh. Look, I'm not even a Cubs fan. I just don't like you, so don't say shit to us, okay?"

That's the best I can come up with? Mr. Rude Jude, Mr. Get Paid to Talk Shit on *Jenny Jones*. All I can do is explain how my accent stems from my place of origin? I blame the Vicodin.

He keeps on talking and I'm staring him down like, "I'ma fuck you up." But he knows I won't, so he stays on me. Now I'm arguing with him and I'm not very good at it, but I can't stop and my friends are telling me to chill.

He's still calling us douche bags and calling me all types of wiggers and shit. He keeps on yapping, and I can't shut him down. I'm getting owned by a frat boy at the Dodgers game, and it's irritating the shit out of me.

The only thing left to do is punch him in the face, but let's be real, I'm not a fighter. I'm worried about my glasses. I'm not about to start fighting, doped up on Vikes, wearing a maxi-pad, at a goddamn baseball game.

I try to get his wife to chill his ass out. "Can you please get your man? Ain't you embarrassed?"

She says, "You should be embarrassed."

This bitch.

Then I see my opening. What I see on her thighs and what she sees every day when she gets out of the shower . . . I see some cellulite on them fucking thighs. Now me, I like cellulite, it don't bother me. But I know she hates it.

So I say something to him like, "Blah blah blah, look at

the scoreboard, loser, fuck you blah blah blah, with your chubby-ass wife."

And his face breaks and I see it, so I keep going. "You need to stop rooting against us and start rooting against her eating all them hot dogs at the game cuz she's getting fat, bruh."

I found that soft spot. And now his homeboy jumps in like, "Whoa whoa, we don't need to be talking about people's wives."

Where were you five minutes ago? I ignore him and keep calling her fat and he keeps trying to say shit back, but it doesn't matter what he says, cuz I keep on disrespecting his woman and his honor and he's not doing a fucking thing. Ain't shit to do but punch me. I might be a bitch and not wanna fight, but guess what? He's a bitch, too, and I'm gonna remind him.

Now I'm pointing at my mouth smiling.

He says, "What the fuck is that? All I see is an ugly red beard."

I say, "That's me smiling. I live in your head now, motherfucker. Cuz you know your wife is getting fat and every time she gets seconds on some food or gets dessert and you tell her not to . . . you'll be thinking about me."

It's true. He'll be thinking about me when he sees that cottage cheese on her legs and when she's on her period, feeling fat, and he'll have to reassure her. That's me, motherfucker. And I bet you she won't be wearing those shorts again anytime soon.

You shoulda seen her face. You shoulda seen her put that popcorn down. Fuck her. That's what she gets for being married to a douche bag.

And now he ain't talking as much and his wife is whispering for him to just calm down and to drop it and it's okay and she knows she's not fat.

I'm sitting in front of them sipping my lemonade, smiling, watching the game, bleeding into my maxi-pad.

animal planet

LORI TRIED TO BLOW ME IN Jamaal's basement after the homecoming dance. I wouldn't let her. I was afraid of pussy and thought my dick was too small. I didn't want her going back to school talking shit.

I told my homeboys, "I ain't let her to do it cuz she was a ho."

They was like, "And?! That's who you sposed to let suck your dick!"

They're calling me all types of lames. I pound a forty of beer. "Let's run some spades."

I was a fat fucker. Some fat kids are okay being fat. I was the one who wore his T-shirt in the pool like I was fooling somebody. I was a chump. I'd sit on the phone with girls I liked and listen to them complain about how their man was dogging them; I was waiting in the wings while they stayed with him.

When I was little, my mom used to take us with her to go cheat on my dad. He cheated first, but we didn't know that. My sister and I would be in some guy's living room sitting on the couch watching Hall and Oates on MTV while she was off in the bedroom doing whatever.

Years later I watched her hold down a bunch of jobs to support her deadbeat-ass husband. He'd be laid up on the couch, hungover with his sunglasses on, watching *The Young and the Restless*, talking to her like she was a fucking gerbil. And she'd take it. I used to beg her to leave, but she wouldn't, and after a while, I'd be like, bitches ain't shit if my own mom's this dumb.

Over the next few years I started dropping weight, pulling more chicks. It was Valentine's when I finally got some ass. I met her at McDonald's and banged it out in a church parking lot, made it halfway through that Des'ree song and nutted all over my Nautica shirt.

I dumped her a few months later. Her ass was so flat I'd get mad when she bent over. She'd be in front of the TV changing the channel, ass looking like a cookie pan.

She'd be like, "What's wrong, Jude?"

I'd be like, "Nothing, take me home."

After that, me and Loc would try and run girls. I'd be getting head in the laundry room from some chick and he'd show up with his dick out. Most of the time, they'd look up at me, mouth full of penis, like, "Really?"

But every now and then, they'd suck us both up.

One time we were riding in the car. Me, Loc, and his girl in the middle.

He looks over to me and whispers, "You gotta rub her."

So I throw my hand between her legs, start rubbing her

pussy through the jeans. The whole ride back from Seven Mile, I was on her. They drop me off and she's mean mugging.

Loc gets out, he's like, "Ay, you got that shit, cuz?"

I say, "Got what?"

He says, "You got a rubber?"

I said, "Hell naw! That's what you was askin'? You got a rubber? Man I thought you said, 'You got to rub her'!"

We're laughing about it. She's in the backseat salty.

We were some dogs but where we lived, it was Animal Planet and the chicks were no better. Ben's baby looked an awful lot like Jermaine. Melody put Pooh's kid on Jamaar cuz she found out Pooh was fucking his retarded sister.

Dont was claiming a son for two years, then went and got a blood test right before the kid's second birthday. Wasn't his. Canceled the party, took the gifts back. Never saw him again.

We all had told him that bitch wasn't shit. She used to borrow Dont's car and we'd see her other baby's daddy driving that bitch down Perry Street. Told Dont about it, he ain't do nothing, so we clowned his ass, too.

Years later I asked him why he dealt with that shady bitch. He told me cuz he didn't think he was good enough for anybody else.

I get it.

Roach used to cock-block. He'd get the neighborhood whore and turn her into his girlfriend. We'd be about to run a train on this chick. He'd get the pussy, then block the doorway talking about, "Me and Krista spoke on it, dog, and it's just gonna be just me and her."

Fine, we'll run her purse.

Next day, he's like, "That's fucked-up, you didn't have to take her beeper man."

And we'd be like, "You didn't have to wife our fuckin' busto."

One time I had this drunk chick in the bathroom about to blow me, but her big cousin kept knocking on the door, so I told Roachie, "Take her ass down to the graveyard while we keep her cousin busy, and me and Myron'll meet up with you in like ten minutes and we'll all get our dick sucked."

He didn't even go to the graveyard. By the time we found 'em under a tree somewhere, Roachie'd already gotten some head and was talking to her about her boyfriend and she's sittin' there crying.

We're standing over her arguing.

Myron's like, "What the fuck you do to her? Why the fuck is she crying? All you was sposed to do was take her down the street and wait for us."

"Yeah," Roachie said, "but we just got to talking about her man. She started crying. That's it."

Myron says, "That's it? Man, we all trying to get our dick sucked, why you talking about her man?"

She's bawling under the tree talking about how she misses Mikey or some shit. I go over to her, take my dick out, and tell her, "Put this in your mouth; it'll make you feel better."

She starts crying even louder.

I put my dick away and we leave her there under the tree.

maps of africa

MY LAST BED WAS HAUNTED. IT was my dad's bed when he lived in LA. He got it from someone else, and when he went back to Detroit, it was mine. I lugged it around town with me from apartment to apartment. I dragged it along.

I fucked my homegirl on it. The next day, when I was cleaning up the mess, I peeled back the sheet to see a mattress pad covered in stains. She called them types of stains "maps of Africa." Like if you fuck someone so good, you leave wet marks on the sheets that look like a map of Africa.

That's what I'm left with: maps.

I've forgotten half the women who contributed to my mattress. They've moved on, got boyfriends, and forgot about me, too. But their marks are still there.

I stood in the bedroom of my new apartment, the one I was supposed to have gotten with Julie, wet towel in my hand, sopping up this mess I made with somebody else.

I thought back to an argument Julie and I had had. She

was sitting on that bed in Burbank, we were yelling at each other. I was hurt about some lame she had slept with when we were broken up. People are gonna fuck who they're gonna fuck, but some failed rapper turned real estate agent I knew from back home? She couldn't have fucked an astronaut or somebody worthwhile? She had to fuck a lame from my area code? I was mad she told me about it, I didn't need to hear about that shit, but since she did, I was grilling her. Where, when, why? How many times? She sat there silent and defiant.

I said, "Fuck it, I don't give a fuck who you fuck. You think I care who you fuck? I don't give a shit. You know how many girls I fucked right there where you sittin'? Right there, in that spot, where you sleep every night? You laying in that shit."

She sat there arms crossed on the edge of the bed, right where I had bent over some black hooker and fucked her on her period. Something in me was happy knowing that. She acts like she don't care. I know she does.

I was looking at those stains on my bed. My dad's bed. Thinking about that fight. Looking at all that DNA. Thinking about what a cruel thing that was to say to someone I love.

I didn't wanna be able to say that to my next girl.

I got a new bed now. I'll make new memories.

I saw Julie at Target today. She's lost weight. She was buying travel-size soap and toothpaste. She was reading the labels and didn't see me. I didn't want her to.

I turned around and left the store.

I thought about where she might be going with her travel-size toothpaste.

I pushed that out of my mind, told myself to harden the fuck up.

ahab

EVERY TIME I GO TO FLINT, I end up at LLT's, this grimy little strip club on Saginaw. They do a five-dollar lap dance, and I know you shouldn't go bargain hunting for your tattoos or sex workers, but I just can't turn down a good deal.

In my defense, you'll understand that five bucks isn't as cheap as it sounds. Flint's like Detroit except it's smaller and shittier. It looks like they built a shantytown, dropped bombs on it, and then moved people in. So five bucks in Flint is like ten bucks in Detroit. It's the Tijuana of the Midwest.

As plants close and jobs leave Michigan, LLT's has been a good barometer of how hard the recession has hit. The first time I went there in '99, I got a lap dance and a hand job from a cute little Filipino chick who would've been a ten if it wasn't for the birthmark on her face. Last Christmas they had a girl with Down syndrome working. She had on a Coca-Cola sweatshirt and a hip pack. I didn't get a dance from her, though; I got mine from a black chick with a bullet wound in her back. Times are tough.

Six months later and I'm back in town, looking to stimulate the economy, throw some money at these broke chicks, get my dick grinded. It's the day shift, about 98 degrees, the AC's broke so they got the back door open with a box fan in it, daylight coming in. It smells like the carpets haven't been vacuumed in months. Some old white dude's on a Rascal chatting up a fat redbone playing the touchscreen with a Newport 100 dangling from her lips. The one security guard working is sitting in the middle of the bar getting a lap dance.

The dancers are murderers row: one's Wesley Snipes, another's a carny, the redbone looks like a glob of peanut butter. I get a dance from a forty-year-old meth head with a half-shaved Mohawk and a ponytail. But fuck it, she's a grinder and has a good attitude. I give her a fiver and keep it moving.

I'm shooting pool when this haggard broad comes up to me with a sob story about her baby daddy in prison. I buy a dance. She calls herself Tweety. I think she's Mexican because of the brown C-section scar on her belly and the knife wound on her shoulder. She's got a tattoo of her baby's footprint on her neck and another one, prison style, in the middle of her back, off center, that says GOOD MOM in block letters.

I ask her how'd she get the knife scar.

"Fighting with my old man."

Of course.

Her skin's saggy, the dance is lackluster, and I'm losing interest. It's always the begging-ass strippers that give the shittiest dances. That's why they're begging.

And then I see her, from across the bar in all her majesty, tucked in the corner, grinding on some pathetic chump. My Moby-Dick, a white girl with dreadlocks and an ass like a Clydesdale. She looks like a Robert Crumb drawing straddling his knee, pushing her thigh into his groin, Nine Inch Nails banging away. *I wanna fuck you like an animal. I wanna feel you from the inside.*

And what's that I see? Could it be? It's too good to be true. . . . She's only got one arm.

This chick is Goth as fuck.

I want a dance off her ASAP.

Years to come when I'm at the bar and some dipshits are telling their little pussy-ass stripper stories, I'm gonna be able to hit 'em with the "One time, up in Flint I got a lap dance from a one-armed stripper."

And everybody'll be like, "Whoa!! What the fuck!!?? You're fucking crazy!!!!"

And I'll take a sip of my water with lemon and say, "Fucking-A I am, fucking-A."

I give Tweety five bucks to leave me alone and I wait for the one-armed Goth.

The song finishes and he pays her for another, then another; it's like time's crawling. Jesus Christ it's stuffy in here and fucking hot.

The redbone's eating BBQ chips, pushing her ass up

against the old dude's dick in the Rascal. We lock eyes; she's chewing.

I order a Coke from the bartender; it's flat. I drink it anyway.

Three songs later and the one-armed Goth's done. She's walking toward the ladies' room. I cut her off.

"Excuse me, I'd like to get a dance from you."

"You want it out here or in the champagne room?"

I ask, "Where's the champagne room?"

"That chair in the corner."

"Here's good."

She sits me in a chair off to the side and gets to it. What I didn't take into account was the sweat she worked up dancing five songs straight in 90-degree weather. She's got a good lather going and it's dripping all on me. I watch it pool and run and drip and she's dragging her slimy ass all over my shorts.

Her arm stops after her elbow in a pointy nub that collects sweat like a stalactite. She rests it on me to get balance. I'm horrified, more by her constant sweating than her nubby arm, but the nub's not helping and she's rubbing it against my arm and I can feel her bone through the skin. I thought it'd be mushier. I wanna be a champ, I wanna ride this out. But I'm feeling kind of fucked-up, like is this what it's come to? You're getting lap dances from one-armed strippers to impress assholes you've yet to meet at a bar you haven't been to?

My shorts look tie-dyed from the sweat, her slimy little nub's on my neck, and all I can smell is smoke and dust and her fucking Victoria's Secret body spray.

I need to dead this shit right now, but if I do, she's gonna think it's cuz she's handicapped. But they wanna be treated like regular people, so, if a regular person's sweaty nub was rubbing all over me, bumming me out, I'd tell 'em. Except a regular person wouldn't have a sweaty nub arm. Catch-22. Where do we go from here?

I take a deep breath and stop her. "You know what, honey, that was a great dance but I gotta get going."

And right after the words come out of my mouth, the song finishes. If I would've waited five more seconds.

She wipes her forehead and fakes a smile and says, "Yeah, okay."

I'm faking a smile back, forcing eye contact. "Naw, it really was."

"It's okay."

I give her a ten, tell her keep the change, and walk straight out that bar into the light.

straw dogs

I'M DRINKING BUBBLY WATER OUT'A PLASTIC cup, staring at a black gas can and black cassette tape mounted on the wall trying to figure out why I should give a fuck.

It's some dude's art; it's supposed to be about Islam. The Ka'aba, it's a black stone they pray on or something. I don't know. Seems to me it's just an excuse for this guy to show off all the cool black things he's accumulated over the years. Oh look, there's an accordion, how very.

I wanna punch this dude in the throat. I'd do it if I knew he wouldn't hit me back. As a matter of fact, I wanna punch everybody in this room, all of them, with their designer eyeglasses and hipster haircuts.

How the fuck did I travel to Berlin, halfway around the world, just to end up in fucking Williamsburg, or Silver Lake, or Wicker Park or wherever the fuck the cool kids go nowadays, listening to the same music, having the same conversations and looking at the same shitty art on the wall?

I coulda stayed in the States, I coulda gone back home, but this is what I asked for. Cultured white people. I got it.

I used to spend my holidays in Detroit with the family, but I started resenting them. I'd drop all this money and all these vacation days to fly out and see these motherfuckers, and these selfish fucks couldn't get their shit together for one day. They'd show up late or bring their asshole boyfriends along, and I'd end up arguing with my pop over some bullshit.

I come back for Christmas one year, my aunt's got this Hindu crackhead motherfucker sitting on the couch, drinking a forty out the bag, watching a bootleg of *Ghost Ship*, talking 'bout, "Aw hell naw, brotha, I know you from *Jenny Jones*. You used ta give dem girls da bidness!" Fast talking, trying to get me to drop some money on a bottle of something good.

Him and my aunt are wearing matching dashikis with the hammer pants and neither one of 'em is black. This dude fixes curry for Christmas. We're fucking Italian, man. Don't sully our table with some fucking vindaloo. But I'm a good sport, I take a bite. There's a hair in it.

I'm not even mad at him, I'm mad at my aunt for bringing this jive-talking Hindu around me. A week later, he ends up stealing her Volvo.

My last trip, I spent Christmas in Peru. All I wanted to do was sit on the beach, play rich American, and fuck top-notch whores at third-world prices. I ended up hiking up mountains looking at ruins and shit, and if you seen one ruin, you seen 'em all. It's rocks on the side of a hill. I mean, it's cool at first but by the tenth one you're like, "Okay I get it, they had a good thing going with their rocks and sticks and gold, then the Conquistadors came and fucked them up."

At first you try to connect with the little native motherfuckers, on some "help me understand you" shit. But they just beg for money or try and sell you alpaca sweaters. You ain't shit to them but a wallet. When I got home, I found out all my sweaters were fake. So I was like, next vacation, I'm kicking it with the conquerors. White privilege.

So here I am with these expats and Germans and it feels just like America. I'm pressing my homegirl Krista to take us to Poland for Easter, get some of that Eastern Bloc, Iron Curtain flavor.

A group of us end up going to her homie Wojciech's family farm deep in the Polish countryside. We take the train in; it feels like some real official communist shit, stark green interior with a lot of BO and cologne. Just how I imagined it.

For dinner they kill a hog and hook us up with ribs and sausage. We drink shots of vodka, toast Wojciech's name day, and Rachel and Kuba dance drunk on the table.

Kuba takes some of us to the local disco, which is basically a warehouse in the middle of a field chock-full of blue-eyed women with childbearing hips and men who look like Ivan Drago. It's nice to be in a place the Internet hasn't ruined yet.

We're walking up, I ask Kuba, "Are there any faux pas with y'all Polish cats I need to be aware of?"

He says with a thick accent, "Don't try to talk to any of their women, don't look anybody directly in the eye, and don't be gay."

"Don't be gay, okay, I got it."

He's fucking with me, this guy. This place can't be that bad—shit, they're listening to a dance mix of Ace of Base's "The Sign."

And then I hear these women yelling and a crowd of men spill out the club, fists swinging. It looks like they'd been lifting pigs all their lives, threw some bootleg Ed Hardy on, and decided to punch each other in the face. They bloody each other up while their girlfriends trail behind, screaming for them to stop.

I walk into the disco, head down.

Based on this place I can tell you three things about the Poles: they aren't fond of deodorant, they're way into black lights and Day-Glo paint, and they really seem to love Ace of Base.

Everyone's on edge, a light bump can lead to confrontation. It feels less like a club and more like the prison yard. We stick around for a couple drinks, dance amongst ourselves, and head back to the hostel.

When I say hostel, it's not like the regular hostel that one might imagine, with a clerk and shit. This was an empty farmhouse in the middle of nowhere with nobody working. The only people there were us and a group of drunk Polish twenty-year-olds who heard there were American girls in town so they came by to check it out.

So Wojciech invites them in for a nightcap. I'm thinking they're his cousins because I had seen a couple of 'em outside his aunt's house at dinner. There's six of 'em: a giant albino with a bowl cut who's about a half a head taller than me, the blackout-drunk guy, three other nondescript Poles (think extras in a bread line), and a bootleg Leonardo DiCaprio.

I hit the bathroom and throw a suppository up my ass cuz I hadn't shit since I got to Europe and the ribs and mayonnaise-based salads got my gut feeling crazy. I figure by the time these motherfuckers get done with their drink, I'll be in the bathroom shitting. I come out to the corridor, where everyone's standing and the albino's hitting on Krista.

Krista's pointing at me saying I'm her man. Now I hate that shit, why the fuck do I have to pretend to be someone's man when it's convenient for the lady? You gonna keep pretending after they leave and gimme a fucking blow job? Didn't think so.

So I'm shaking my head no. "Nope, I'm not her man, she's a lesbian, she don't like dick." Give 'em that lie, leave me out of it.

He moves on to Rachel; Leonardo DiCaprio's trying to hit on her too.

I'm like, "Naw, that's my sister. She's got a man."

Wojciech translates.

They go back to hollering at Krista, with their buddies giggling in the background egging 'em on.

I say, "Damn, y'all over here trying to holler at all our chicks, where's the girls for us?"

Wojciech asks 'em.

The giant albino says back in his little Polish gibberish, "Blah blah blah bordello blah blah."

"Good, let's go to the bordello. I'm on vacation, I'll buy a fucking hooker. Shit, Wojciech, tell your cousins I'll even buy them one. Let's go."

I try and walk 'em out but they're not moving. Wojciech says to me, "They're not my cousins."

I'm like, "What? They're not your cousins? Then how do you know 'em?"

He says, "I don't."

Now it gets real. We're out in the middle of nowhere, in a foreign land, with no cell phones, no nothing, I don't know the language and we're chilling with six semi-aggressive drunk Poles. I mean it's cool right now, it's cool till it's not cool. I start thinking about *Straw Dogs* and mob mentality. Maybe I should've said I was Krista's man.

Krista says she's tired and goes to her room to lay down, but before she can shut her door, Giant Albino pushes in behind her with his three homeboys and Wojciech in tow.

That leaves me outside with Rachel and Leonardo DiCaprio. Rachel's drunk and she's trying to show Leo how to high-five.

She's like, "No no no! That's not hard enough. Here, give me your hand. Give me your hand! Okay, put it up, yeah like that. Now you have to hit it like you mean it like . . ."

Bam! She hauls off and slaps the shit out of his hand. He winces and shakes it off. I'm staring at her like what the fuck are you doing?

"Now do me! Come on, do me."

He cocks back and hits the shit out of her hand and she's nodding, saying, "Yeah yeah, that's right. Let's do it again."

And they do, again and again.

The blackout drunk is holding a bottle of vodka, shuffling back and forth behind them. I'm thinking this might end bad. I'm searching the room for something to hit 'em with. All they have is plastic lawn furniture.

Now she's giving him her five-hundred-dollar camera to play with. Why not?

She wouldn't be doing this if it was acceptable for dudes to punch chicks in the face. I mean they do it, but it's frowned upon. I wish it wasn't. If a chick could get fucked-up just like a dude, they wouldn't do half the dumb shit they do out in public.

I've seen more guys get gut-stomped because their fucking girlfriend was mouthing off to the wrong dude. Look, we wanna be chivalrous, but ladies, you gotta know when to shut the fuck up and act right.

One time, I took this idiot chick out. We're at Denny's after the club and she starts talking slick to some 18th Street Gang motherfuckers at the table next to us. This bitch. We haven't even fucked yet and she's trying to get me into fights.

I'm eating my eggs watching this shit go down, then the one with the tattoo on his cheek calls our whole table some bitches. And now I gotta say something. I'm playing it cool on some grown-up shit, but I'm scared as hell, white-knuckle clenching my butter knife in case I gotta stab somebody in the face.

I say, "Look, we're all adults here. I haven't disrespected you, so let's not disrespect each other. Why don't we just finish our meals like some grown-ass men and be on our way?"

The teardrop cholo looks me dead in my eyes and I look right back at him. Maybe he sees fear, I don't know. Or maybe he sees a man on a date with a nincompoop who's not even giving up the pussy, and is just trying to get out of Denny's without having to fistfight four dudes because of her.

He says, "Fuck it," finishes his omelet, and leaves.

If I'm ever in that situation again, I'll check her ass before it even gets that far. But it's different with Rachel; she's not really talking shit. She's just drunk and not understanding how camera loans and aggressive high fives with intoxicated strangers from Poland could end poorly. Plus she's my sister, so like, I'll fucking ride with her no matter what.

I hear shouts from Krista's room and go check it out. Krista's on the bed with the giant albino lording over her, trying to get a kiss from her, she's telling him no and laughing nervously. He steals one anyway.

I look at Wojciech. I say, "Dude, could you get them out of here?"

It takes another ten minutes to round them up, get Rachel's camera back, and finally get 'em to go. When we're walking them out the albino starts directing his frustration at me, the four-eyed, pencil-dick Yankee who kept him from banging an American girl.

He's pointing at me, talking shit in his language. Probably calling me a faggot.

I'm smiling the whole time. "Okay, whatever you say, I can't understand you, just fucking leave."

Now he's making fun of my glasses and they're laughing

and high-fiving each other. I smile and nod. "That's right. I wear glasses, say it while you're walking, bro. Say it while you're walking."

Wojciech shuts the door. I say, "Man, that coulda ended real rapey. I was thinking we was gonna have to fight them dudes."

"Oh no, they're just kids, it's fine."

"Yeah, okay, just kids. It's all good till it's not all good. I figured I was gonna end up having to get gut-stomped in the corner defending my sister's honor."

We're laughing and there's a knock at the door. It's them again. Their car broke down and they need a push. Six of them and they need a push. Leonardo DiCaprio's behind the door trying to sneak in. I block his way and then it happens. My asshole catches fire. The fucking German suppository finally melts. I'm clenching my butt cheeks trying to keep these dudes out and trying to keep my shit in.

I can't make it. I look at Wojciech and say, "You deal wit 'em, bruh."

He shuts the door on 'em.

I run to the bathroom, drop trou, and explode.

I'm still on the john when I hear another car pull up and then another car. They're at the door pounding on it, hollering.

Boom boom boom! Boom boom boom! Boom boom!

Must've been fifteen of 'em out there kicking at the door. I'm in here shitting my brains out and I'm thinking, you dumb fuckin' Polacks, that ain't no way to get an American girl. You gotta do it with shitty art, hipster haircuts, and designer eyeglasses.

desperado

I GAVE UP SEX, SO I started drinking again. I hadn't drank in six years, so people were surprised by it.

I tell 'em, "I wanna be like *Mad Men*."

They're nodding politely. "Oh."

"Plus I gave up sex, so I've taken up whiskey."

Now I'm explaining myself and they're looking around the room for someone else to talk to. "Fucking all these chicks adds up. I don't know. . . . It's just not where I wanna go in my life. And you can't get a bottle of liquor pregnant. Lord knows I've tried."

Bottoms up.

Andrea thinks I'm doing too many drugs.

Maybe I'll try yoga.

I was tellin' Z, "I wish pills weren't so bad for you. I'd pop them instead."

I used to chow down Vikes and do crossword puzzles. Itching.

I don't even like the buzz of liquor. I like the act of drinking it. I post up at the bar, order my whiskey neat, and sip it. They're selling a lifestyle and I'm buying.

I'm a cowboy.

I wake up with a headache and rotgut. Drink more water next time.

Andrea says maybe I'm depressed and I should take Zoloft.

Fuck that. I'll stick with depression before I take a fucking pill. I'd rather do drugs to escape the weirdness in my head than take a pill to cure it.

Lately, I've been having nightmares. I woke up one night, my bed was shaking so hard I thought I was in an earthquake. Checked it on Google the next day, see what it measured. Nothing. Wasn't no earthquake. That was just me, shaking.

I've been having sleep paralysis, too. I was tellin' my friend Natasha about it. She says the Vietnamese call it "the ghost on your chest." It feels like it.

Ain't shit to do but go back to sleep.

I've been watching documentaries on 'Nam lately. When we were kids, we didn't play cowboys and Indians, we played 'Nam. We'd run around the apartment complex with guns and sticks killing invisible soldiers. Maybe you shoot somebody or maybe you get shot. Maybe you die. I used to like dying. I found comfort in it. Just lie down in the grass with your eyes closed and die.

big red

THERE'S NO YELLOW AS BRILLIANT AS vitamin piss. I got on some latex gloves, fishing out a busted glass lodged in the toilet. There's shitty toilet paper in the glass but no shit in the bowl and I'm grateful.

The bar's empty. I'm alone here in the john. I got a knot of ones in my pocket; they tip me when I give 'em a towel. I got Altoids, too, and I sell cigarettes for a buck a piece. The Arabs bitch about it but they still buy one; sometimes I'll sell a whole pack for twenty.

Tonight this Chaldean fucker tried to steal a pack of gum from me, when he was in there with his boys. They were wearing Armani and silver chains. They had nice watches and stank of cologne. They own party stores and sell cell phones.

They make their money in bombed-out neighborhoods, behind bulletproof Plexiglas in a cage. Detroit doesn't scare them, cuz where they're from, there's tanks and land mines and Molotov cocktails.

Now they're in my bathroom trying to fast-talk me, trying to haggle. The one with the arched eyebrows is gonna steal my gum. It's not about money; he's got money. He just wants to take a piece of me and chew on it, chew on my gum.

He can't have it. I work in the john; how much lower does he wanna see me? Should I know my place? Or does he hate the way I pop my paper towels to people? I tell myself a man's job doesn't define him. I try to prove it.

I see him put the pack of Big Red in his pocket. I sell it a buck a stick, I tell him he owes me five dollars. He plays dumb, there's a confrontation. I won't back down. His boys don't want trouble; they push him out but they don't pay me.

I'm heated, I tell the bouncers. They don't do a fucking thing, cuz last week the Albanians beat their ass and this shit is giving 'em flashbacks. I start packing my shit.

"Fuck that! If I gotta worry about some A-rab motherfucker coming here, stealing my gum and y'all not doing a fuckin' thing, I quit."

So they kick 'em out. Now I'm happy.

I don't know what I hate worse: Saturdays with the Jews and Arabs or Fridays with the fags. Saturdays they wanna fight me and Fridays they wanna fuck me, whipping their dicks out or trying to shove a five down my pants. I don't let 'em, but you can't let 'em know if you're gay or straight cuz if they find out you like pussy, money's gone.

I been here a year now; I'm pee shy and got gaydar. I leave the door open to let the smell out. I smoke Black & Milds, drink bottles of water, and bullshit with the regulars.

Sometimes a girl will walk by the john and recognize me.

"Aren't you Rude Jude from *The Jenny Jones Show*?"

"Yeah, that's right, how you doin'?"

"Why are you working in the bathroom?"

It's a good question. I wonder it myself. I gotta pay rent somehow. The *Jenny* gig pays shit and ain't steady enough to support me. I wanna save up to move to Cali cuz I got dreams to make happen. I'm gonna be in the movies.

When I tell people this, they doubt me. Chasing dreams is scary. And what do you do when you catch 'em? So now I keep my dreams to myself and I tell 'em rent and child support.

I gotta pay child support cuz Assia's damn near five and I haven't been around enough. Her mama says I ain't shit. She's right. I try not to think about it. I send in money and that's it. But it haunts me. I dream about Assia sometimes, about her being old and not recognizing me. When I wake up my heart hurts.

On those days, I try not to look in the mirror. And maybe I get up and fry an egg and smoke on the porch and watch the cars drive by. I'll call up my boys and go to the mall and forget about her.

I stay away for months. I feel so much shame, it's hard to face her. When I finally man up and come by, no one wants me there. Assia ignores me and plays on the computer. I'm stuck talking to her mom. Even when we were fucking, we didn't talk.

She was a booty call. We used to fuck at work, in the base-ment of McDonald's. I'd wipe my dick off with a grill towel, then I'd go flip some more burgers and not say another word to her.

I hadn't even seen her for six months before I found out she was pregnant. She left a voice mail on my pager.

"Jude, this is Tameka. I'm pregnant, call me."

I'm in bed with my girlfriend Maria, and Maria is pregnant, too. We end up killing the baby and breaking up. And now she hates me.

I'm talking to my baby's mama, and she's giving me one- and two-word answers.

"So what's up? How you been?"

"Fine."

"All right, what you been up to?"

"Nothing much."

"How's the job goin'?"

"Fine."

I make up an excuse to leave and kiss Assia goodbye. I drive to work feeling worse.

Now I'm in the bathroom trying to explain to some coked-out JAP why a man on TV is giving out mints for tips.

She's still confused. She asks me, "So do you shine shoes, too?"

I force a smile and shake my head.

"No . . . I don't."

smile

ME AND MY OLD ROOMMATE CHRIS are at some hot new BBQ joint in Williamsburg with Punk Rock Rusty. At first I was skeptical, ready to hate it. Everybody eating there had extreme beards and asymmetrical haircuts. I breathed through it. Hating these trendy motherfuckers is too easy; it's like punching Munchkins. The bottom line is hipsters are people, too, just dumb people. And I gotta tell ya, I got the ribs and brisket, and the meat fell off the fucking bone.

I saw a girl there in a pink jumper getting a jug of beer from the bar. I fell in love. I do this every now and again. I'm like that James Blunt song where he sees a chick on the subway and writes about loving her, then she bails.

This one was pretty—not a knockout, but it wasn't her features that got me. She got me with her smile. It was warm and kind and her eyes lit up when she spoke to people.

She smiled like she'd been loved as a child.

I wanted her to be my girlfriend. I wanted her to smile at

me like that. I wanted her to wake up with me every morning and give me that smile in bed, and kiss me with her hair all messy before she brushed her teeth, before she hopped up to make tea and start her day.

And when I was being grumpy and difficult, I wanted her to smile and say, "Oh Jude, you're being ridiculous."

And melt my heart.

I wanted her to have my kids. I wanted to get her pregnant. She looked like she'd be a good mom with her kind eyes. But what do I know. I just finish my ribs and drink my whiskey like a cowboy.

She was in the doorway when we left. I had to speak.

I said, "Excuse me, miss. Don't take this the wrong way, I'm not hitting on you, I don't want nothing from you, I don't even live out here. But lemme tell you, you are the most beautiful woman in this place. Just take that for what it's worth."

She looked taken aback at first and then she smiled at me, with her mouth and with her eyes. And it felt as good as I thought it would. I walked away wishing I would've said something more. Something clever, something heartfelt, maybe ask to call her. But I didn't. I said what I said and now it's off to see Brad in Bushwick. It's the new Williamsburg.

The bar was on Knickerbocker and Troutman. The block reminded me of seventies New York in the movies, with the people on the stoops and the girls in their little shorts popping bubble gum talking to the guys hanging out the window.

Cars drove by with their Puerto Rican flags and loud music. They had Puerto Rican flags everywhere, on the porches, on the roofs, all over. I saw a motherfucker walking down the street with a flag tied around his neck like a cape, on a Wednesday.

I'm laughing with Chris, saying they might as well have been white flags, it's over for 'em. Cuz if I'm in your neighborhood coming for specialty cocktails and a twenty-dollar burger, you might as well give up.

The white people are coming, and where we go, death and destruction follow. Death, destruction, and carrot-apple-ginger juice. I give 'em five or ten more years and then it's a wrap for Bushwick as we know it.

After a few hours we head home, the gypsy cab drops Chris off and I go up to midtown for a couple more drinks.

It's damn near three, I'm heading back to Chris's. The streets are empty, just me and the garbage trucks. I see couples staggering out of the bars together, hand in hand. All these couples out here, what do they got that I don't got?

The cabbie's gunning it down 5th Ave. We pass the whore house I used to go to when I lived out here. I feel that ping in my chest. I almost tell him to stop, let me out, but I don't. We drive on by.

I tell myself, I don't need that in my life. The cramped room, fucking some Korean whore laid out on a towel. She's fake moaning her way through it, stinking up the joint with her kimchi breath—trying to get me to cum fast. Don't worry sweetheart, I will. I don't last long with hookers, and when I'm cumming, I look in their eyes and hope they smile. They never do.

karma chameleon

I WAS WITH ROSS THE OTHER day. He tells me it turns out Karma Patel, the billionaire heiress, Harvard grad, cancer patient he hooked me up with a few months back, ended up being a little teenager named Lauren.

I figured as much. I knew she was lying the minute Ross told me that in the year knowing her through Facebook, he had never actually met her. And when I pressed her to meet, something always came up.

But I figured all of this out days—and many phone conversations—after our first introduction. I had been speaking to her like she was a dear friend of one of my oldest friends, honestly and candidly.

Ross had cosigned for a bullshit girl.

We turned Hardy Boys, Ross and I, trying to crack the case. But every lie we caught her in would turn into a bigger, more elaborate lie.

"Oh you're gonna be here at six?"

Five o'clock she's in a car wreck.

"Where?"

"Santa Monica."

"The street or the city?"

"Both."

"Where by?"

"Can't remember, the brain cancer pills cloud the memory."

"That's awful. Which hospital you at? I'm coming to see you."

"Just got out, heading home."

"That's even better, I'll check on you there."

"No you can't, chemo in the morning."

"Great, I'll take you and hold your hand the whole time through. Okay?"

"Okay."

Five in the morning, emergency brain surgery.

And so on.

Why would a normal person take time out of their busy life to entertain this obvious bullshit? Well, in Ross's case he had a year's worth of correspondence put into this and he wanted some answers. Me, I'm not normal, I'm abnormal, I'm a fucking nut. I do weird shit. I was mad I got duped, I felt my trust had been violated, and I just wanted to catch her in the act. Call her out, ask her why.

I wanted to be like, "Exhibit A, people do not get metal plates put in their head from brain cancer! Exhibit B, there were no said Karma Patels brought into any hospital in Los Angeles on said date! Exhibit C, the land deed to 662 Maryland

Drive is under the name of Bob Jones and not to any Patell!!! I got just one question for you, Karm. . . . Stop crying, Karm, it's okay. I'm not mad, I'm just disappointed. Just answer me this. . . . Why'd ya do it, Karm? Why'd ya do it?"

I was playing that conversation out in my head as I drove over to 662 Maryland Drive, got out of the car, and entered the gated property. But while I was in the backyard, peering into the window of a sitting room completely abandoned save for a cardboard box (a light rain drizzling on my head), it dawned on me: Maybe I was taking this a bit far. Maybe there is no "why." Maybe some people are just assholes. And maybe I was turning nutty once again.

Growing up, at least once every year, I'd just snap. I'd hold shit together all year long, then something would set me off and I'd get arrested or fight the police or fight my principal, or get expelled or have some nervous breakdown.

And as I was losing it, I'd know in my head I was doing something extremely dumb. But I'd just keep going, because I had to. I couldn't help myself. I had to see it through.

As I've gotten older, I've learned coping mechanisms to deal with stress, like jogging and breathing and doing drugs and shit like that, and these episodes have since waned.

Standing there in this stranger's backyard, on that fresh-laid sod, peeping into a window that wasn't mine, it hit me. I was a cunt hair away from one of these episodes. I stopped. I looked around the backyard at the half-dug pool, at the shovels lying in the mud, at the rain-soaked plywood on the ground next to it.

I stopped and said out loud, "Jude, you've lost it again."

I then walked away from that house, from out their back-yard, out the gate, got in my car, and drove to the V Cut cigar lounge for a cup of tea. I blocked all her calls and never attempted to contact her again. I was back to normal.

Later that week, Ross told me he saw on Facebook that she died of brain cancer. I guess the emergency brain surgery couldn't save her.

Rest in peace.

We didn't really speak on her till months later, at the Tar Pit over whiskey.

Ross is smiling. He's like, "Judo, I gotta tell you something."

"Yeah? What?"

He goes into this whole story about Karma and how she got busted lying by some Canadian rapper; she pulled the same shit on him and he got a private investigator and Ross reached out to the dude. ". . . and then, they tracked her down to her house in Maine or Vermont somewhere. Peep this: turns out, she was just some little teenage girl named Lauren getting over on all these rappers. Case closed."

I'm shaking my head. I say, "Hell naw. She was a teenager? That British accent had her sounding old as hell. She sounded like the BBC and shit."

Ross is like, "Young as hell, Judo. A teen. A baby."

I say, "I was on the phone with her a bunch. I phone-sexed her. I phone-sexed a fucking fifteen-year-old? Goddamn."

He says, "Yup, probably, I don't know how old she was. She was a teenager, that's all I know."

"Where she from again?"

"I don't know, Vermont or something."

I say, "A motherfuckin' teenager."

Ross is like, "Yeah . . . you phone-sexed a child, Judo."

He's laughin'.

I'm still shaking my head. "Goddamn. Now that I think of it, she did cuss a lot for going to Harvard."

"You ain't bust, though, did you?"

"Huh?"

"With the phone sex, you ain't cum right?"

"Naw, naw, I faked that shit. I ain't cum. I acted like I did; just trying to get her to bust so I could go to bed."

He's like, "You're good then."

We're quiet for a second. I say, "I wonder if she faked cumming, too. She lied about everything else." I look at Ross; he takes a drink. "She prolly faked that shit. That little lying motherfucker." I take a drink. I say, "Ross if I couldn't even get a fifteen-year-old off with my phone sex game, I just don't know what I would do."

I crack a smile. I'm just kidding . . . kind of.

willie

THE ITEMS IN MY SHOPPING CART are the following:
one leek, one large carrot, a cucumber, one Chinese eggplant, condoms, lube, maxi-pads, toilet paper, and wet wipes.
I impulse-buy some energy drinks at the checkout and head to
the crib to wash up. I just finished yoga.

The porn chick on the show today is a little white girl with
a big round ass and a large black following. We're playing a
game called "Guess What's in Me." I'm on the mike trying to
be clever and put condoms and lube on the vegetables at the
same time. It's not easy. I shove the lubed-up veggies into her
pussy one at a time and work them around for a bit. She's
blindfolded and has an industrial-strength vibrator on her clit.

She's spot-on, she knows her veggies. I fuck her with the
Chinese eggplant till she cums. Listeners love this shit, the
phones are going crazy. I don't even get hard. It's just a job.

Porn's ruined for me. Ignorance is bliss. Sometimes lies are
better than the truth. When they listen, they're thinking about

her cumming, I'm thinking about herpes. I'm thinking about big dicks pounding dry pussies and fake moans.

We sit in awkward silence and wait for the song to finish to go back on the air. Not much to say after you just threw some vegetables up a stranger. She tells me she used to watch me on *Jenny Jones*. I tell her that's cool. She tells me her friends never heard of me. We take calls. I thank her. She's sweet. Show's over. I'm off to bus tables.

It's what I do for fun. I'm Andy Kaufman. When people I meet find out I bus, they think I'm poor. "Radio doesn't pay well? It's tough to make ends meet, huh?"

I wish I could let it slide, but I tell 'em, "I do well, I'm just slumming it."

It's a joke. Some laugh; others don't. They think I'm talking down. I came up doing this shit. My mom was the help, I'll make those jokes.

My real job is to sit in a box by myself talking shit. It's nice to be around people and move. I ain't slumming it.

I know this chick, a Harvard lawyer who fucks Mexican busboys to feel part of the struggle. I hate that bitch. She's slumming it. Yeah, I wanna fuck immigrants, too, but it's more about the movement of their ass in them sweatpants walking down Vermont, pushing a stroller. Their willingness to let you cum in 'em speaks to the inner caveman in me. Fuck the struggle; they can keep their fucking struggle.

I'm driving to work down Pico checking out a Mexican chick walking, baby in hand, one in the stroller, a tamale away from being overweight, ass swinging. I'm listening to Willie

Nelson in the car, like my dad used to do. He'd bang around town in the maroon Chevette, smoking Kools, singing along with Willie, *You were always on my mind. You were always on my mind.* Take a drag, blow that shit out.

They put him in the loony bin around that time. Him and my mom are arguing, phone rings, it's the guy she's seeing, she takes the call. Pop goes bananas, he's hollering, breaking shit. Cuts his hand open on a busted jar. It's long and deep, he's bleeding everywhere. Drives himself to the hospital for stitches and they admit him.

I'm on the porch sharpening Popsicle sticks, staring at my dad's blood on the concrete as he rushes off.

Days go by. I ask my mom where my dad is.

"He's sick. He's not feeling well."

We go to the hospital to see him. We're outside in the visiting area by the pull-up bar with the wood chips. He's sitting at the picnic table, somber. He looks like a man who just lost.

He told us about the rape years later, when I was ten or twelve. We were going to my Nonnie's in the Buick and he laid it on us. Rachel and I were playing in the bathtub when it happened. They were still married but she wouldn't fuck him anymore; she said she wanted to be faithful to Darryl. So he put a knife to her throat and raped her.

He said he did it for love, said the knife wasn't that big, said he was drinking and drugging. Said he got crazy when she started seeing that other guy, his head just broke. He said he lost it.

Well, that cleared things up. That's why Mom showed up

to Nonnie's that day trying to take us from him. That's why Grandpa slapped him in the face. That's why she wouldn't let him in the house anymore and he'd always try to come in anyway.

Knife wasn't that big, he said; it was more symbolic.

The very next breath, he'd say, "Look at this, we're alone, she did this to us! She broke up our family. Ya all I got left; all we got is each otha! We gotta be good to each otha."

And he'd clutch the steering wheel, sobbing, and we'd nod and comfort him.

And when I was in the car with my mom, I'd say, "Mom, why'd you break up our family? Why'd you do this to us?" She'd never say anything bad about my dad and I'd just stay on her till I saw tears fall from her eyes and something in me liked that.

He joined AA to get her back, said it was the alcohol that made him act that way. Didn't work. He ended up just fucking the rehab chicks. No one was buying it anyway; it takes commitment to be a drunk and he lacks that. He's no drunk, he's just crazy.

He'd get mad when my ma's people wouldn't invite him to Christmas. Every year it was the same thing. "Oh, that broke dick Darryl is invited and not me? He's not even family! Ya own fatha isn't welcome? That's bullshit, that really hurts. You gonna let them do this to ya own fatha? Ya not gonna stick up for me?"

Till years later, finally we were like, "Well, goddamn, of course Darryl is invited, he didn't rape Mom."

His eyes'd well up and he'd start mumbling shit and then he'd bring it up again the next year.

I'm in my car now, thinking about Julie, all our fights, all the times I spazzed out and punched the walls, how I scared her. How I'm my father's son. Thinking about how I could've done things better. Singing along with Willie, *You were always on my mind. You were always on my mind.*

coop-coop

JINX USED TO FUCK AROUND ON Shae all the time. We'd be coming from some chick's house and Shae would beep him and we'd have to go get her a corned beef sandwich from the Coney.

She loved those sandwiches. He'd show up with a corned beef smelling like some other bitch and she ain't never say shit.

Jinx and Dont got caught fucking some hood rats. Turns out one of the chicks was Shae's cousin. He never met that one, lived in the same city and everything. Bad luck, I guess. Jinx blamed Dont, said he set it up and talked him into doing it.

I don't think Shae believed him, but she made herself. She wouldn't let Jinx and Dont hang out no more. Dont was real hurt off that.

We're talking about it years later. I tell him, "What you expect? He was in damage control, that motherfucker got a kid wit her. That's his wife. You think he's gonna sacrifice all that to stay boys wit you? Shit, man, come on."

Dont would plead, "Yeah, but that was out cold, he cut me off. He just cut me off. We was boys, Jude, we was all boys. You don't do that to your boy."

Yeah, we was boys, but Jinx was Jinx. He was the same motherfucker that'd try to put his dope up under my seat when we'd drive around town.

I'd be like, "Jinx, get that shit from out under my seat, man, or I ain't getting in the car."

"I ain't finna put it under my seat, what if we get pulled over? They gonna blame me. I'm black."

"They gonna blame you cuz it's *yours*."

I'd remind Dont, and he'd be like, "Man, I miss that dude anyway."

Growing up, we used to bang chicks for shoes, shirts, their car, money, anything. See who'd get the most.

I did all right with the rich black girls. I'd get some Perry Ellis or Nautica cologne. Jinx'd pull the hood rats and maybe get some Jordans out of them. But Jinx's half brother Myron was the best at it because he got the white girls. He'd tie a bandanna around his head backward and they'd say he looked just like Tupac.

That motherfucker ain't look shit like Pac; he just looked like a black dude with a bandanna around his head. But the white girls from Clarkston loved it, and they were the cash cows with the redneck dads. So he'd be Pac. He'd get their money and they'd get to piss off their family, ruin Thanksgiving, and see about a black dude's dick size.

Jinx'd say Myron didn't have the game for black chicks.

Myron'd say that Jinx's mama poked holes in the condom and that's how she had Jinx.

So Jinx finally got his hooks into this white chick, but she was broke and she was ugly and stayed in Pontiac.

He was like, "Come on, we finna fall through to Bethany's house. She got a cousin—you wanna roll wit me?"

I was like, "The one Jamaal used to fuck? With the glasses?"

He said, "Yeah."

I say, "What for? That bitch is ugly as hell."

"Cuz I'm 'bout to go coop-coop. Get breaded, buy my mama something for her birthday."

Coop-coop meant fuck in Jinx talk.

We get to this run-down house on a back road behind a liquor store. It's winter and the trees are bare and the snow is gray and the street is empty. Bethany's waiting in the doorway, storm door steamed up from the cold. I can't see her glasses or her face but I see the outline of a dumpy girl and I know it's her.

We roll in and barely speak. Jinx takes Bethany to the bedroom and leaves me with her little cousin. I sit there and talk with her about junior high school while Jinx and Bethany fuck in the next room. You can hear her hollering over the rap music.

I ask the cousin to show me her room; she says she can't cuz they're in there fuckin'. But she could show me her mom's.

She takes me to the back of the house, to a filthy room that smells like cigarettes and dust, with wood paneling and clothes on the floor. Hot pink bandannas are tied to the bed-post with a faded leopard-print bedspread thrown across the mattress.

I sit on the bed, tell her to come here. I kiss her on the mouth awhile. I tell her to get on her knees and take my dick out. She does.

"Put it in your mouth."

She does as I say. I finish in her mouth without telling her. She's gagging and spits my cum all over my lap. I wipe it off with my hand and smear it on her mom's leopard blanket.

I say, "Thank you, you're good at that. Excuse me a second, I'ma get Jinx."

I get up and leave the room and pound on the bedroom door for him to hurry up. He's taking forever, fucking her like he's got a point to prove.

Five minutes later they come out. We're all posted up in the kitchen.

He asks Bethany for the money. She says she doesn't have it.

He's like, "Bethany, why you gonna have me come over here and you know you ain't got no money. Why was you lying? You knew you ain't have no money."

"I wasn't lying, Jinx, my aunt had needed to borrow some to put toward the light bill—"

He cuts her off. "That ain't got shit to do with me. You said you had something for me to hold for Mama's birthday. Why you have me come all the way over here when you didn't? You think I'm coming here for free? How'm I sposed to buy my mom a present?"

She's apologizing. "I'm sorry, I had just gave it to her right before you got here, Jinx, I swear to God."

It's getting kind of weird; her little's cousin's fidgeting. I'm like, "Come on, man, fuck it. She ain't got no money, let's just go."

She says, "I get my check next Friday; we can go cash it together."

"What I'm sposed to tell my mama? Wait till next Friday for her present, cuz you had to pay the light bill? Fuck that."

He starts looking around the kitchen, all three of us watching. No one's talking. He's looking in the fridge, looking on the table, looking on the counter.

He goes to Bethany, "Unplug that—I want that."

I look over and he's pointing at the most busted, run-down toaster ever. Aluminum, dents in it, a crooked lever.

She's like, "You want the toaster?"

"Yup."

Little cousin starts pleading, "But that's my mom's toaster."

"And?"

"I don't know. . . . You can't have my mom's toaster. That's our toaster. . . ."

Bethany's trying to console her: "Don't worry about it, I'll buy you guys a new one on Friday. When I cash my check, we'll go get you a new one."

I'm feeling kind of fucked-up. I mean the little girl just headed me off, I wiped cum all over her mom's bed—now we're 'bout to take her toaster? I'm like, "Jinx, man, come on, son, let's just go."

He walks over to the counter, pulls the plug out the wall, wraps the cord around the toaster, tucks it under his arm, and heads to the door, crumbs spilling all over the place. Bethany rushes after him trying to kiss him goodbye; he moves his head.

I look at lil cuz and say, "Sorry about your toaster."

Arms crossed, looking away, she don't say shit.

We're at the car and Bethany's hollering to Jinx, "Call me Friday, okay?!!"

We get in. I look at him, say, "Hell naw, dog . . . you wild for that one. You just fucked that ugly-ass broad for a toaster."

He's smiling. "I know, I'ma give it to my mom, she ain't got one."

"Well . . . knock the crumbs out that bitch 'fore you give it to her."

His pager goes off and we head on over to the Sonic to get Shae that corned beef she wanted.

relapse

SHE CAME OVER THAT NIGHT AFTER work, drunk. I gave her Irish whiskey and fed her steak.

I told her we couldn't fuck, I'm fasting.

I told her I lose interest in a girl if I smash too soon.

She told me she'd never heard it called smash before.

She told me she was on her period anyway.

I'm a Viking. I told her periods don't bother me.

We end up on my bed, making out. It gets heated.

"Let's chill."

We do.

I fall asleep and wake up to her kissing my neck, rubbing my dick.

I bought a new bed because of nights like this. Fucking to fuck. I was trying to keep the new one DNA-free. It was gonna be my little gift to my future girlfriend—an untainted bed, like a born-again virgin.

Then it dawned on me: that's gay as fuck. Sure, the whole

celibate-till-you-meet-the-right-girl thing would be nice, but it's not practical. It's just leaving me horny. I'm developing a porn addiction and a rash around my dick from jerking off with cocoa butter.

I hadn't smashed in two months and I was about to ruin the bed. I guess we could've fucked on the couch, but I don't trust the legs on that thing.

Fuck it.

I kneeled above her, lifted her skirt and yanked off her panties, took my shirt off, and put it under her ass. I pulled out her tampon and threw it behind the dresser. Unwrapped a rubber, put it on my dick, and fucked her.

She lay there on top of me, with me still in her, panting.

It was good.

My Jordan shirt's ruined.

She hopped in the shower.

I washed the blood off my dick in the bathroom sink.

We went to bed and fucked again in the morning.

When I came I looked at her like, what have I done?

I'm telling her, "We shouldn't have done that. I don't know. . . . We shouldn't have done that."

Why the fuck did I do that?

I see how this is gonna end. How many of those "let's keep it light" talks am I gonna have?

After a while, it's never light.

She's consoling me for banging her, like I'm the girl. Patting my shoulder, telling me it'll be okay.

She says, "It wasn't casual sex; there was nothing casual about it."

Whoa.

I stop her. "How gay is this shit? I'm good. I'm sorry, that was fun. I had a good time last night."

She leaves for work.

I get out of bed and make tea.

Drink it on the couch and say to myself, "Oh Jude, what am I gonna do with you?"

choppers

AS A TEEN I WAS HAVING problems with my molars. I hadn't been to the dentist since the fifth grade; we didn't have insurance.

We were "the working poor," barely making rent, missing it some months. That health shit's a luxury when you're scraping by.

Both my parents had bad teeth, so it was important for us to keep our shit clean.

Every time my old man would have another problem with his mouth he'd call me over to his dresser in the living room and pull from the top drawer a mason jar with six yellow rotted-out teeth in it.

He'd bring me close and shake the jar in my face, teeth clanging against the glass and start yellin'. "Look at dis! Ya know what dis is?! These are my fuckin' teeth, this is what happens if ya don't brush ya teeth! Brush ya fuckin' teeth!"

I'd roll my eyes. "I do, chill out. . . ."

"Oh you do?" He'd stick his finger in his mouth, pull back his cheek, and expose gaps where his teeth used to be. "Look at that! All ya got is ya teeth! Brush ya fuckin' teeth! Or you'll end up like me!"

I brushed my teeth, but they got fucked-up anyway. I guess I shoulda flossed more.

My ma saw some ad in the paper; a new local dentist was charging sixty bucks for fillings and a cleaning. She got it in her head that she was gonna take me there.

I didn't take her serious; she was always making plans. Like, we should go hit an art exhibit or take a nature hike before school. We never did.

My mom worked three jobs; we'd get up late; my stepdad Terry would be out all night in the van and bring it back on empty. We're just trying to get to Mobil before we run out of gas. Put thirty-seven cents on pump two and get to Rochester.

We get home, my mom's been working all day. Terry's on the couch, hungover drinking a Rolling Rock, watching soap operas with his sunglasses on. There's nothing in the fridge to eat but some cold cuts, and he wrote his name on 'em.

We ain't never take that nature hike.

For weeks she'd be like, "Just wait, when I get my check, we'll go to the dentist. We'll get your teeth cleaned and fix that tooth for you. And maybe we can get lunch before that, too."

I'd be at the kitchen table with a toothache nodding. "Okay, Mom, sounds good."

"And Jude, once you get your teeth fixed, you'll be starting new, and then you can take better care of them. Because you

have to take good care of yourself; you're the only self you
have."

She even had the little coupon from the paper saved,
folded up neatly.

A few weeks pass; she gets her money up and makes the ap-
pointment. I take a half day off of school. It's spring. It's sunny
and breezy. You can feel it in the air, it feels hopeful.

When the weather was like this, my old man used to say,
"It's days like this makes me happy I didn't kill myself."

We'd laugh and say, "Shut up!"

We pull into the brand-new strip mall. Our van's beat-up but
we're wearing our nice clothes, and my mom's commenting on
how nice the parking lot looks with its new painted lines.

She's excited to be doing this for me. She's happier than
I am.

We roll up into a full waiting room, I sign in, fill out the
paperwork, the little dental hygienist lady takes me to the back.
I'm sitting there in the dental chair with my bib on. My ma's
back there with me, too.

They're being real nice, with the how-ya-doings.

"Do you want some water?"

"Yes, please."

And in comes the dentist with a hi-de-ho and what can we
do for ya?

He's sitting on the stool talking to me. I tell him where it
hurts.

The lady from the front desk comes back with a folder and
pulls the dentist aside, they're talking in hushed tones.

Then the dentist gets serious; he asks my mom how we're gonna pay for it. My mom's got the cash in her hand, sixty dollars ready to give to him.

He tells her it's not enough. He's pointing to my forms, telling us how we don't have insurance.

She shows him the ad. He tells her that ad's for people with dental insurance.

He points at the fine print at the bottom of the coupon she's holding. He tells us how much it's gonna be, it's like four hundred dollars. It might as well have been four thousand dollars. We ain't have it.

My ma's standing there with the coupon in both hands. Her face breaks. Her eyes well up.

The dentist is thanking us for coming in and asking us to leave.

I hand the hygienist my cup; she won't even look at me. They undo my bib; I get out of the chair. We walk down the hallway, past the receptionist, past the people in the waiting room, and we walk out.

I keep my chin up, but I'm embarrassed and she's mad. Mad she ain't see the fine print and mad they put it on there so small.

We just wanna be normal.

We're in the parking lot and she's shaking her head, muttering. We look like someone just stole our bike.

I put my arm around her. I'm like, "Fuck them, Mom, I'll be fine. Fuck them coupons wit they fine print and shit. My shit ain't even been hurting lately. I'm good."

She nods. "Yeah. Fuck them."

"His breath stank anyway. No-chin-having motherfucker. How the fuck you gonna be a dentist with some stanking-ass breath?"

We laugh about it, hop in our van, and drive off on that sunny spring day.

the predator

I'M AT A PARTY HOUSE IN Hollywood to grab some 2C-E from my dubstep, death metal, computer nerd homies. It's a designer drug, psychedelic. I've never done it before.

They're telling me they snort it and hit the water park. It feels like you're cumming when you go down the waterslide. The body buzz is that good.

I tell 'em that's creepy.

Johnny's like, "Yeah, I was in the kiddie pool with a boner and didn't realize it. No one told me."

"That you had a boner?"

"No, that I was in the kiddie pool."

We're laughing. "Hell naw."

The art school junkies on the couch stop watching cartoons long enough to give us a dirty look. Fuck them and fuck skinny jeans. I cop five capsules. I shoulda bought more.

Paulie's like, "What are you going to do on it?"

"What I always do. Fuck."

Johnny's like, "That'll be awesome. Better have her get the morning-after pill. You're not gonna be able to tell if you came or not it feels so good."

"I'm straight—I'ma rock a condom."

They look at me like I'm retarded. "A condom?"

"Trust me, as many fucking abortions as I've been through? I always wear a condom."

I end up doing it that Saturday with a girl I was seeing. I was helping her look for an apartment, then we had some dinner. I throw the 2C-E on a plate, chop that shit up, and we go for it.

She's nervous, she never tripped before. Lately, whenever I do drugs it's with a beginner cuz all my old drug buddies went and joined AA, got married, or grew the fuck up. I gotta walk her through it.

I say, "Snort that shit."

"You first."

Fair enough. I roll up a five, cuz I'm on a budget, put it to a line, and blow it up my nose. When I was a kid, me, Dre and Roach chopped up some lines of sugar, wanting to be like the drug dealers on *Miami Vice*. I went first. I sniffed that shit and started sneezing and coughing and spitting. After me, they ain't want none.

That's what the 2C-E felt like. It burnt like a motherfucker. My nose is running and my eyes are watering. I don't know if I have to puke or shit. I tell her to do her line, I'm going to the bathroom.

I'm on the toilet, and I start hearing echoes but nobody's

talking and the walls start breathing in and out. I got this picture of Jesus and he's staring at me while I shit. It's fucking with me.

So I start talking to the picture like, "Hell naw, Jesus, I'm fucked-up."

He don't say shit back. I gotta get out of here.

I come out and she's sitting on the couch, nervous talking. "The rug looks like water."

I tell her, "It ain't water, you just trippin', relax."

When doing this with a rookie, one has to appear totally confident to help them be more comfortable with their trip. I tell her to chill the fuck out and be cool. I leave out the fact that I was talking to a picture of Jesus while I was shitting.

I'm like, "Just pretend like you're on a raft and you're floating down a river. You may see some shit you like and you may see some shit you don't, but just remember it's not permanent, it'll change. Just go with it."

She chills. I shoulda been a motivational speaker.

I go and snort some more, cuz it seems like the right thing to do.

M83's on the iPod. I feel the burn. I look up and see sound waves.

It looks like that movie *Predator*, when the Predator uses his super-alien camouflage and goes damn near invisible and starts fucking people up. He looked all wavy on that shit. That's what the music looks like, it looks like the fucking Predator. The Predator's in my house, chilling above the lamp, by my ficus.

I say, "Aw shit. I see the song."

"Me too."

"It's the fucking Predator. This is fun, ain't it?"

She says, "Yeah, real fun."

We watch the music for a while out in the living room, Coltrane and Debussy and M83. We close our eyes and each song takes us to a different place, a different time. I'm in a speakeasy somewhere in the South listening to Coltrane. Air's got me floating down a river and the sky's orange from the setting sun. I watch music notes dance through my head to Debussy.

We hit the bedroom and fuck for a while. I eat her pussy to M83; it's epic. I don't use that term lightly. I'm not the guy talking about a Meat Lover's Pizza claiming epic and shit. I'm eating her pussy with fucking beams of light shooting out of my head. I wanna send M83 a thank-you note.

I take a Viagra, cuz that's what I do: I do drugs, eat dick pills, and sport-fuck. It works for me.

The songs feel like they're going on forever. I gotta keep checking my dick to make sure I didn't nut.

We're taking a breather. I say, "Wow! These drugs are so much fun!"

She's like, "Oh my gosh, you sounded so white just then."

I stop. I say, "I am white."

She looks at me all earnest and shit. "You should just be yourself. You don't need to put on a front, just be yourself." Silence. "You don't have to act all tough. My friends read your blog. They tell me what you say."

Her friends think I'm some tough-talking wigger. Some of my own friends think that shit. You should see the chicks they try and hook me up with. They think I'll jibe with some fucking dental assistant because she likes Dr. Dre and drinks Hennessy.

I decide not to touch it. I'm keeping it light tonight. I didn't snort this shit to discuss how her fucking foodie friends view me.

She won't stop. "You know, in college, they put me in an all-black dorm. I was around all the black kids, so we've got more in common than you might think."

I go, "Oh yeah, we got a lot in common, huh? You hung out with black people in college? What school you go to again?"

"Stanford."

I'm laughing. "Stanford, huh? I got a feeling that your black people are a lot different than my black people."

I don't give a fuck if she came up around black people. I respect her cuz she put herself through school.

Coltrane comes back on the shuffle, and I'm right back on the bayou at sunset and I'm kneading her ass. I like this drug.

We fuck for hours, till she's bleeding. Fucking condoms. I guess we needed lube. I take off the rubber and we fuck some more and when I finally do cum, I cum buckets—in my hand, on her belly, it's dripping on the sheets.

We drink some water and eat some Xanax, and I go to sleep praying that she remembers to take that morning-after pill.

crazy sexy cool

THE FIRST HIGH SCHOOL GIRLFRIEND I ever had looked like TLC. When people ask which one, I say, "All of 'em."

I was fifteen when I met her. I'm on the bus coming back from Adams High cuz they didn't offer Black History at my school and I'm taking Black History because of course I would take Black History. I see her sitting up near the driver looking out the window, looking good, caramel complected with perky breasts. It takes a couple days to get the nerve up to speak, but I do. Her name's Kit. I get her number, I call her that night.

We talk for hours about nothing, about everything. She likes cartoons. She likes birds. She's always like, "Look at the birds, Jude, look at the birds."

I crack jokes, and sometimes she gets 'em. When I get off the phone, I'm like, "All right, I'ma hit the road."

She says, "Don't hit the road, Jude, don't hit the road."

I'm smiling; she likes me; I never had no girl like me before. "Oh, you don't wanna get off the phone, do you? You like talking to me, huh?"

"Don't hit the road, Jude; you'll hurt your hand if you hit the road. Why you wanna hit the road, Jude?" I'm like wow, this chick's an idiot. Or maybe she's a genius. I was just watching on the Maury Povich show how they got these chicks that act stupid but are really smart just so they can get over on the doctors they date.

I'ma keep an eye on this one, make sure she doesn't ask me for money or anything. She never does.

So we're going steady. I never see her at school, only the bus ride back. We sit together, I rub on her leg with a little hard-on in my pants; the bus driver's always giving me dirty looks. Fuck her; what's she know about teenage love.

I finally got a girl. I'm not the fat funny sidekick anymore. I'm not Chris Farley, cracking jokes for everybody then drinking by myself when they couple off.

Sometimes my old man'd even drop me off at her house, and I'd suck her titties in the kitchen while her mom and stepdad watched *Wheel of Fortune* in the living room.

This goes on for a couple months, when her stepdad pulls me aside. He's like, "You know we moved out here from Detroit because the boys were teasing Kit so bad. She'd come home crying every day."

I'm shaking my head. "Naw, she never told me that. Kids can be cruel sometimes."

He goes on: "It got to the point where I had to wait at her bus stop just to make sure them boys left her alone."

I sigh. "It's always the pretty ones that get picked on."

He's looking at me like I'm stupid. "Jude, you never noticed anything different about Kit?"

"Naw, just that I like her a lot."

He says real slow and low, "You know, Kit's mentally challenged."

"What!? Naw!" I'm laughing. "Come on."

"I'm serious; she's got the mental capacity of a third grader. I just thought you should know that, so you'd do the right thing."

"Hrrrrm . . ." I'm nodding, thinking back.

That bus we took home together was kind of short . . . and it did have tinted windows . . . and a chairlift. She did like birds an awful lot. . . . Holy shit. My girlfriend's a retard.

That very next day, I did do the right thing. I broke it off with her. It got out that she was slow and people had jokes for me, but how the hell was I supposed to know she was retarded? She wasn't drooling or anything; she's not like retarded retarded.

Three years later, I've dropped fifty pounds, finally got some pussy, started dogging hos and I see Kit downtown at some festival. She's with her sister buying a hot dog.

She still looks good, midriff showing, pants saggin' with the panties out, looking like TLC and shit. I'm thinking if she was like a third grader three years ago, her brain's probably in sixth grade by now and her booty looks like it's in college. Maybe I can fuck. I get her number, tell her I'll call her sometime.

A few weeks later, me and Jinx are doing mushrooms.

We're driving around Pontiac tripping balls, trying to holler at bitches, but none of these chicks are messing with us cuz we're a little too fucked-up.

We're coming down and we're sitting on the truck looking up at the stars talking about the universe and the meaning of life.

Jinx is like, "I need some pussy."

"Shit, me, too. You got anyone?"

"Just them girls we saw earlier."

We were gonna try and fuck with these little hood rats who lived in the Knolls, but we had to leave cuz Jinx's hands had turned into pyramids and started spinning.

Then I remember Kit. "Hey, I got somebody we can call, and she got a sister."

"How she look?".

"Like TLC, dog."

We're at the pay phone. I call her, say we're coming over. Her mom's gotta give me directions cuz Kit doesn't know how to get to her own house. I tell her to make sure her sister's awake. She says okay.

We get lost, it takes an hour to get there, it's 1 A.M. by the time we show up. Kit comes to the door in a prom dress, a pink velvet gown with one shoulder strap and sequins along the sides. On her feet are house shoes.

She's alone. I say, "Where's your sister?"

"She upstairs."

"Well, go get her."

"She busy."

"Doing what?"

"Sleep."

Tough break for Jinx. Being the wingman, sometimes you hit the jackpot and sometimes you crap out. There's been many a time I had to babysit some gorilla-looking bitch while Jinx got a blow job. So he's gonna be riding this one out on the love seat, solo.

She puts a movie in the VCR. "Jude, have you ever seen *Friday*? I love *Friday*."

"Yeah, let's watch that shit."

She's crouched in front of the television trying to get it to work. On TVs back in the day you had to have it on channel 03 to play movies. She keeps pressing channel 30. 3-0 static. 3-0 static. 3-0 static.

Finally I say, "Hey, babe, you gotta put it on three for the picture. Press zero-three."

She says, "Naw, I do this all the time," and starts flicking one channel at a time through the dial. She gets all the way to channel 80, gets frustrated and presses 3-0 again.

Jinx is like, "Aw hell naw!!"

I say, "Hey Kit . . . Kit . . . Hey Kit."

"What?"

"Fuck that movie, just come over here and kick it with me." She stands, TV still on, snow on the screen, sound buzzing, and sits next to me. I say, "Girl, we been here like fifteen minutes, I ain't seen you in forever, ain't you gonna gimme a kiss?"

She looks at me and says, "Naw . . . I'ma play my keyboard." She reaches up underneath the couch, pulls out a Casio, hits the demonstration beat, and pretends like she's playing it. She's staring at us smiling the whole time, moving her fingers over the keys. "I'm good at it, Jude. I'm good at the keyboard."

Jinx is staring at me like, what the fuck? I won't even look at him. "Yeah, you're great."

"Y'all wanna see my gerbil?"

Jinx is like, "Naw, I don't wanna see your gerbil. I'm scared of gerbils."

"Don't be scared of gerbils. I have a nice gerbil."

"Naw, I'm good—don't bring out no gerbil."

She drops the Casio, song still playing, goes in the kitchen, comes back with a gerbil, and tosses it on Jinx's lap. "See, it's a nice gerbil, don't be scared."

It lands on him and runs up his body. Jinx is hollering, he jumps off the back of the love seat, the gerbil goes flying and scampers across the carpet and under a chair. Kit's on her hands and knees trying to fish it out.

Jinx half mouths, half whispers, "Dog. This bitch is crazy. Let's get the fuck gone."

I whisper back, "Hold up, man, I'm trying to fuck."

"Jude, man . . . Come on."

"Gimme ten minutes."

He gives me this real disappointed-dad look and just shakes his head.

Yeah, it's one in the morning and I'm trying to fuck a retarded girl wearing house shoes and a prom dress trying to catch a gerbil. So? I bet that ass ain't retarded. I ain't say shit to him when he fucked the cripple.

I say, "Kit, let's go in the kitchen. I think the gerbil ran in there."

I get her to follow me and that's when I put the moves on her, in the kitchen in the dark. I'm kissing on her and she keeps talking about the fucking gerbil. I'm rubbing her titties and it's gerbil-gerbil-gerbil.

I'm hiking up her dress, and she's like, "Jude, what are you doing, Jude?" Then I put my hand down her drawers and she's saying, "Jude, that feels funny, Jude. That feels funny."

I'm like, "Hold up, I got something for you." I take my dick out. I touch her pussy and it's dry as a desert. Then it hits me. Usually when I do my moves their pussies are pretty wet by now and her shit is not wet at all. As a matter of fact, it's probably the driest vagina I've ever felt in my life. Maybe the experts are right, maybe she is all the way retarded—like retarded retarded.

I place my penis back inside my trousers, pull her dress back down, and excuse myself. There's a gerbil in this home that needs finding, I better leave her to it.

We make our way out and she stays in the kitchen looking for her pet in the dark. Jinx is clowning. I'm just shaking my head, speechless. And when TLC's "Creep" comes on the radio Jinx turns it all the way up and we're laughing.

say anything

I MET THIS CHICK ONLINE A few years back. We'd talk every now and then. I told her if I ever got to Vegas, I'd holler. I ended up out there for work around Valentine's Day. I hit her; we met at a bar in the Bellagio. She showed up with two gay guys; we had drinks and chatted.

They wanted to go to some bar off the Strip and rage.

I told 'em, "Go ahead." I didn't come out for that.

I pulled her aside. I told her I liked her friends, they're cool, but I didn't call to see them, and I didn't call her to run around Vegas and get drunk. I said that we could run around Vegas, but time is precious and soon my time here would be done and maybe we should focus on our wants instead.

She shook the dudes and came back to my room with me.

We turned the lights off and fucked in the dark. She was Rubenesque and moved well in bed. I liked the way her ass felt in my hands and I liked the way she kissed me. She came, and then I came. I got out of bed, threw out the condom, and washed my dick in the sink. Her homeboys were already on their way to get her by the time I came out the bathroom. We kissed and said our goodbyes and I never saw her again.

The Strip is a soulless place. Every time I go there I feel alone. The worst kind of isolation is when the city's buzzing around you and you're totally disconnected. But what am I gonna do? Put on a shiny shirt and hit Tao, drink Coronas, and try and meet people? I usually end up high on some shit roaming the hotel lobby at 5 A.M., looking for something to fuck. I spent a week in Vegas once, shooting some black exploitation movie where I get ate by vampires.

My last night there started off with my homegirl Tina drinking Grand Marnier, and ended up in the backseat of a Malibu with some strippers, driving to a titty bar on the city's outskirts. It's eight in the morning and these chicks are doing bumps of coke off house keys listening to Nelly, while the people in the cars around us drive to work.

The strip club was dead, just a pimp posted at the bar with his two girls working the poles. He's trying to sell me pussy and crank. I took a cab back to the hotel. Picked up a meth head playing video slots in the lobby, took her up to my room, hid my money in my sock, and fucked her with my shoes on. Then put her out when I was done. Later that afternoon, when I finally flew out, I looked over that desert city and it felt like I was leaving 'Nam.

Fuck Vegas. Soulless shopping mall of a city.

So when Sirius told me I had to hit Vegas on Valentine's Day for work, I wasn't that stoked.

Valentine's usually sucks for me anyway. I've had friends killed on that day and dates ruined.

One year I even got fucking VD. Neither one of us was cheating, we were just having dirty sex. Apparently you need to rock a condom for anal and pee afterward or things can get infected.

Who knew?

Every year, being the hopeless romantic I am, I put stock into Valentine's Day and use it as a benchmark to measure where I'm at in my love life. This is bad, cuz I'm usually single or on the rebound. The last place I wanted to be on that day, rebounding, was fucking Vegas.

But that's where I was, so I figured I'd just fuck a girl and make the best of it.

I woke up from fucking the Rubenesque chick, V-day, at noon. Feeling like shit. All the pussy in the world can't mend a broken heart. I dreamt of Julie the night before. I could go all day and not think of her, but she lives in my dreams.

I got up to take a leak; there was blood on the toilet. There was blood on the towel next to it. I looked at the bed and there was blood there, too—the sheets, the pillows, blood. Crime scene. I guess she started her period and didn't know. My bloody Valentine. Here I am in Vegas, trying to fuck the pain away, and I'm covered in blood.

I turn on the TV and *Say Anything* is on. John Cusack and Ione Sky. I love that movie. Julie never saw it. I had always wanted to show it to her. I thought she'd appreciate it, but we never got around to it. I never showed her. I lay in my bloody bed and watched John Cusack chase his girl to the very end and thought about everything I didn't do for mine.

the i.e.

I'VE BEEN DOWN OFF THAT 2C-E for like twenty minutes, had to turn off the trance. I can tell when I'm sobering up cuz trance goes back to sounding like shit again.

I take Ashly to the couch to smoke weed and listen to records. She's twenty-two. I call her the Midlife Crisis. Fucking her is like buying a Corvette and a gold chain. She's closer to my kid's age than mine. She's straight out the Inland Empire. It's nothing but cholos, tweekers, and dirt bikes out there.

The other day she told me I was flitty for ordering a Jamba Juice.

I'm like, "What the fuck is a flitty? I don't speak I.E."

She sighs. "*Flitty* is 'gay,' it means you're fucking gay for drinking a smoothie. We eat our fruit whole. We don't blend it and put it in cups, fool."

I say, "It's a smoothie, it's sposed to be blended. Girl, we gotta get you some culture."

That's what I'm doing on the couch, giving her some

culture. I got her looking at a book of R. Crumb drawings. I'm telling her about him, telling her how he likes fat asses and big legs, how he liked to get piggyback rides from women.

I tell her, "He woulda loved you."

He would've; her ass is fucking nice. I just had my face buried in it, tripping my balls off. The only time she really lets me eat the pussy is when she's high, and even then she puts the blanket over my head so she won't see me.

I got a head cold. I'm blowing my nose then snorting K up my good nostril before it clogs up again. I can't breathe anyway, so colds really mess me up. When I was down there, I was mouth breathing, damn near passing out.

I'm thinking about getting the surgery done. I was talking about it with Z the other day at the Fred Segal Cafe, where the rich and beautiful come to eat organic greens overlooking the parking lot. And then they go buy over-priced bullshit from the boutique.

Right now the fad for guys is to spend a thousand bucks to look like a romanticized version of the working class. I fucking hate rich people.

I'm having my tea talking to him about my nose. I'm telling him how I'm damn near passing out when I'm doing my exercises and how hard it is to go down on chicks.

I tell him, "My septum's deviant and it's fucking with me. I think I'ma get that surgery."

This Afghani motherfucker, been here twenty years and still sounds fresh off the boat, says, "You should, cocksucker, and while you're knocked out have the doctor take a chisel and chip off that big hump on your nose."

"Fuck you, Z, I ain't making my nose smaller. This a motherfuckin' Roman nose!"

He says, "It's not Roman, it's just fucking big."

I point at my nose, I say, "Look, bruh, I'm half Italian. Back in the day, this is the first thing you saw when you was about to get fucked-up, this big-ass Roman nose bending the corner. If you saw this shit come around the corner, you knew two things: one, you was about to get fucked-up, and two, you were about to get some aqueducts!"

We laugh about it. Deep down inside, like most of my non-white friends, Z has a special hatred for the White People's conquests, so I try to bring 'em up as much as possible. He's telling me the Romans were a bunch of fags who fucked each other.

"And? So? Y'all got fucked up by a bunch of queers."

This waitress walks by and chimes in: "Your nose isn't Roman. My nose is Roman."

He says, "See, cocksucker, I told you it's not a Roman nose."

"You think you're right because the waitress agrees with you? She's a fuckin' waitress, she brings me ketchup. What the fuck she know about noses?"

I go to my computer phone to look up Roman noses, which I hate doing. You start talking about anything and some dipshit goes straight to Wikipedia on his iPhone before you can even figure it out for yourself. Well, now I'm that dipshit.

I read off the following: "'A Roman nose is a human nose with a prominent bridge giving it the appearance of being curved or slightly bent.' Now what, motherfucker? My nose is bent as hell. I told you it was fucking Roman."

He just rolls his eyes and shakes his head and says, "It's not Roman, it's just big."

"Fuck you, Z."

Now I'm on the couch putting a rolled-up dollar to my Roman nose wishing this cold would go, and Ashly and I are talking about her liberal use of the word *nigga*. When we met, she was dropping *nigga* all over me. I'm about to introduce her to Ross, and I tell her don't be dropping no *niggas* when we're around him.

We're over at Ross's, she's on her best behavior, and there's some drunk Mormon chick who's all, "Gimme some more Jack Daniel's, nigga!"

Ross doesn't hear it, he's too drunk, but MLC from the I.E. does and she looks at me and rolls her eyes. Then the Mormon goes into the bathroom and makes out with Ross's wife.

Back in the car, Ashly's talking shit. "See, fool, you thought I was gonna say nigga and that dumb blond girl said it instead! All the time you were worried about me!"

"Yeah, I was worried about you; I'm fucking you, I'm not fucking the Mormon."

"Dude, you're crazy. I wouldn't say nigga in front of a black person!"

Her mom was the same way. When I first met her, I walked into the garage. She's in there holding court with her sixteen-year-old daughter's little friends. They're smoking weed and cigarellos, drinking Cold Duck. The neighbor's sitting in a lawn chair; she's got a bloodied bandage on her shoulder.

This little white girl with braces lights up a Black & Mild and says, "Oh, you're Rude Jude. I heard you got jokes, let's have a snapping session."

I tell her I'm off the clock. I look at the bloody Mexican. "What happened to you?"

The mom jumps in, "Aw, fucking Booshie attacked her!" Booshie's their giant dog. "Yeah, we're all sittin' here, drinking and shit and fucking Booshie just loses her shit and hops on Marisol, starts biting her. I fuckin' throw my drink down and jump on her. I'm punching her in the face, yelling, 'Booshie, stop!' Shit, for a minute there, I thought she was gonna attack me! Didn't she look like it?! Didn't she?! We thought Marisol was done for the night but here she is, drinking with us, tough little bitch."

And they all nod in agreement and the neighbor don't say shit, she just takes another drink of champagne out her Dixie cup. Then the mom's like, "Aw shit, I don't wanna do this, but lemme just say, Rude Jude, I fuckin' love you!! I used to watch you all the time on *Jenny Jones* and I'd be thinking he's a funny nigga! This nigga is funny! Lemme get a hug!"

I go over there and hug her and she pushes her fake boobs into my chest and I'm smiling. I'm on my I.E. shit.

eating out

GROWING UP, I DIDN'T GO OUT to eat much. Early on in the divorce, on the weekends, my dad would take us to Mc-Donald's for chicken nuggets, then we'd hit a movie or something, but we never went to sit-down restaurants.

I remember when I was fifteen, Mo took us to T.G.I. Friday's, me and Loc didn't know how to act. We ordered water with lemons and made lemonade at the table using sugar packets. I ordered a chicken-fried steak and sat there, pissed-off when it didn't come out fast enough.

Mo was Loc's big cousin; he got in some trouble in the city and came out to Auburn Hills to lay low. He'd take us all around, buy us dinner, and order the most expensive shit on the menu.

He put us up on game, like how to pull a bitch by tellin' her bullshit, how to give her the danglin' eye, and how you shouldn't fuck the chick super-good till the second time you smash, things like that. Mo was the shit. I loved the fuck out of Mo. He'd do some crazy shit, like if his car broke down, he'd leave that bitch on the side of the road and just go buy a new one.

Mo moved back to Detroit and got shot. Me and Loc kept going out to eat. We'd get our little checks from McDonald's on payday and hit up Murdock's for jazz night, eat fried cheese sticks, smoke Black & Milds, and undertip the waitress because we didn't know better.

When we got a little older, we'd hit Friday's on the regular. I ended up pulling this waitress from out of there.

She was this cute little corn-fed white girl from somewhere in the middle of Michigan. She had just moved to the big city and was living on her own, waiting tables and fuckin' black dudes. She had a thing for black guys, but she fucked with me anyway because I looked good in the face.

We kept it light. I'd see her at her job, we'd smash here and there, but that was it. She hit me up one day and was like, "I need a favor."

A few months earlier, she was fucking with this CBA ball-playing cat. He got her pregnant and bailed. She'd been hounding him for some help and he finally sent her some money for an abortion, but she needed me to take her.

I'm like, "Cool, I got you, no worries."

I stay the night, because I'ma take her to the clinic in the morning.

I wake up the next day wanting to fuck, because I know I won't be able to smash for like a week once she handles the little ball player in her belly. I'm kissing on her, but for some reason she's not in the mood. She's like, "Quit it, Jude, I'm tired."

I'm like, "You just woke up, girl, how you gon' be tired?"

She's like, "Come on, we gotta go soon."

I whisper, "Girl, why you so grumpy? Lemme just do this. . . ."

I start going down on her. She's like, "Come on, Jude stop. . . ."

I put my finger to her mouth. "Don't say nothing, I'ma make you feel all better."

I'm down there licking away, trying to get her in the mood, but it was smelling kind of foul.

I keep going. I come from the school of pussy eating where if the shit tastes bad, you just eat past the taste.

I'm down there for like five minutes, and it's only getting worse. It tastes like fish and pennies.

I quit; I stop eating and start fucking. She's not into it. The smell's caught in my beard and my dick goes soft. I hop off, I'm like, "Come on, we got places to be."

The ride there's silent. She's annoyed I tried to fuck her on her abortion day.

It's wintertime, the sky's gray, the snow's gray, it's a good day for it. The clinic's on the east side in a strip mall somewhere in Sterling Heights. We roll up, she signs in, the doc takes her to the back. I take a seat, crack a magazine. I'm reading, it's gonna be a minute. She comes out ten minutes later, looking stuck.

"That's it?"

She's like, "Yeah. You ready to go?"

I'm like, "Damn, that was fast."

She says, "I didn't get one. . . ."

I say, "You didn't get one? What, you keeping it?"

She says, "No. I had a miscarriage . . . this morning."

I wipe my mouth.

"Oh."

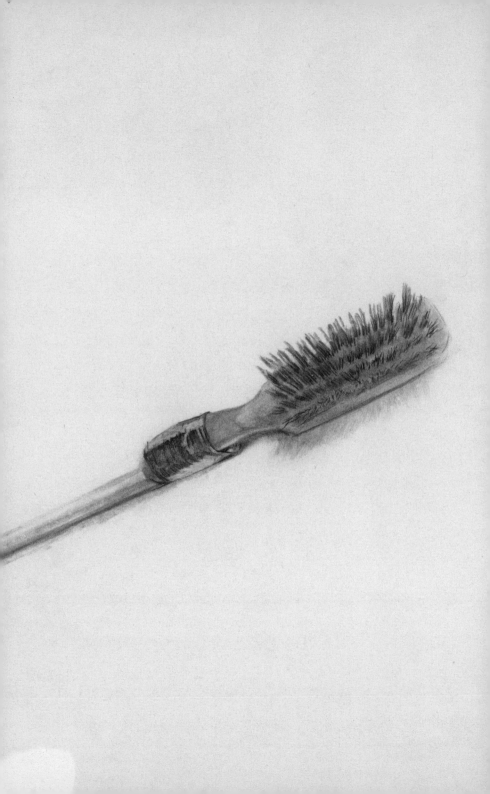

supercuts

I USED TO GIVE MYSELF HAIRCUTS. I'd climb up on top of the bathroom sink, get in the mirror, and chop away. My grandparents hated it, but my aunt's first husband, Rick, loved it, thought I looked New Wave.

When I was around seven or eight, my pop started taking me to Mario's over at the Meadowbrook Village Mall for my cuts. He used to hook it up, cut a part in my hair, finish with some talcum powder. I liked going to Mario. I grew up with blacks, Mexicans, and white trash, so it was nice to be around an Italian every now and then.

Mario knew Madonna's father from the old country, so my dad thought that if Mario gave Madonna's dad his head shots, he could in turn give 'em to Madonna, and she'd hire him in a movie or, even better, wanna fuck.

For months after he gave him the pictures, my pop'd be at the house claiming, "When Madonna sees those pictures of your old man, she's gonna wanna help me out. She's gonna wanna give me work. Or you know what else? She might even like your daddy."

And we'd be like, "Madonna's gonna be our stepmom?! Cool!!"

He'd be standing there next to the dresser, scratching his back with a hairbrush taped to a stick, smiling, saying, "I'm a good-looking guy. It could happen, it could happen."

Mario never gave Madonna's dad the pictures; he didn't feel right doing it. But Pops kept hounding him till one of the other barbers finally blew up: "Look, it's a little weird, okay? They go back a long time and he's not just gonna start passing out pictures, trying to get strangers work. It's just weird."

My pop stood there looking all hurt, said, "Oh I'm a stranger now? You're not even Italian, what do you know, you pencil dick?! He forgot where he came from. Jude, come on, let's go."

After that, whenever we drove by the Meadowbrook mall, we got to hear about it. "That white-bread Italian fuck wouldn't fucking help me. He's jealous I'm an actor and he gives haircuts."

When I was in my twenties, I had Billy-54 cut my hair. He was the doorman at the hottest club in Ferndale. It used to be a Rite-Aid. He'd hook up the ill highlights à la 'N Sync. I swore I had 'em first but no one believed me. We ended up being friends. I even took him to *Jenny Jones*. He wore a zebra-print trench coat on the train and people thought he was a rock star.

When Gabbie and I broke up, I'd sit there in his chair spilling my guts, telling him how fucked-up I was over her. He'd shake his head and tell me he felt for me.

Turns out they were fucking the whole time during the breakup. When I found out, I didn't even fight him. I just wrote a rap song about it and played it for him, like a bitch.

I couldn't believe she'd do that to me. "Out of all the people you can fuck, Gabbie, you gotta fuck my hairdresser? You gotta fuck Billy-54? He wears a fucking zebra coat for Christ sakes. Who the fuck's sposed to cut my hair now, Gabbie?"

I dumped Billy, got back with Gabbie, and made her tell me everything about it. Was his dick bigger than mine? It was. How many times? A bunch. Did he fuck better than me, when, where?

That's why when I met Julie, I was afraid to hit on her. She did such a good job cutting my hair that if it didn't work out I'd have to find someone else.

When we started fighting, I stopped liking my haircuts. I got more critical. I blamed her for going bald. By the time we broke up, I ain't even want her touching my head anymore. I just shaved my head. Fuck haircuts.

I hear Julie's on tour doing hair for some rock group. I'm happy for her. When I drive by her salon I pretend she's out of town. I know just cuz you miss something it doesn't necessarily mean it's good for you. I try and keep that in mind as I grow my hair out.

white chocolate

REBECCA TOOK ME TO THIS OBNOXIOUS movie about some rich white lady who feels bad for being rich so she gives money to bums and not to her spoiled-ass kid. And the kid spends the whole movie all mad about being neglected and ugly. Then the rich lady tries to volunteer at group homes but she cries when she sees the retards. In the next scene a little mongoloid is in the bathroom checking on her to see if she's okay. It's supposed to be poignant. The movie ends with her buying her spoiled little asshole kid some $250 jeans.

I said to Rebecca, "Rebecca, why would you take me to see a movie about a bunch of people I hate?"

She's laughing. "Because I knew you would hate it."

"Asshole."

She likes to get me riled up.

I was talking about it to Anthony, the masseur at my fancy-pants chiropractor's office. We were talking movies while I was trying to avoid the fact that the back of his hand was touching my ball sack.

I told him, "The only people who want to watch a movie about a bunch of rich white people feeling bad about being rich and white is rich white people."

He didn't say shit. He just kept working my inner thigh.

The same lady who did that movie did another one about some white people adopting a fat little black girl because her mom was a crackhead or had AIDS or something. I'm sure all my liberal friends creamed their pants over that one. Can you imagine having your very own black person that you rescued from the ghetto as a pet? You get to touch their hair and bring 'em to parties.

Z took me to a dinner party in the Hills last week and I was talking to this white writer lady in her forties. Right after she finishes telling me about her daughter graduating from Harvard, she starts talking about how much she hates white people.

We're in a party full of people dancing around to U2 with their eyes closed, and there's only one black person there and she's Canadian.

I tell her, "Be proud of your whiteness; white people are the shit. We run things."

She's like, "But deep down inside, I'm black. I feel like a black person. I feel it in my bones."

You feel like your ancestors were enslaved, stripped of their culture and traditions, and you're a product of that? You feel black? Black like she struts around her house listening to Miles

Davis, drinking Cabernet, black. Black like she eats sautéed collard greens with her quinoa, black. Black like you blew a black guy in college.

I keep it light. "Well, you look white as hell to me."

She says, "No, I already have two strikes against me as a double minority. I'm a woman and I'm Jewish."

I'm like, "You're Jewish!? You ain't no minority. Shit, that's like being white with benefits! You're like white-plus."

She grabs my arm and looks dead in my eyes. "Yeah, but deep down . . . I am black."

I take a bite out of my wood-oven gorgonzola-and-shallot pizza. Chew it up and swallow it. I let that one sink in.

Man, I think I hate white people, too.

gorilla piss

I GET A CALL FROM SOLO, a longtime listener. He says he can get me some PCP if I can get him some mushrooms. I usually don't do drug deals with people I've never seen, but he calls in all the time and when he talks, he reminds me of my homie Jinx, so I'm like, yeah, what the fuck.

What do I have to lose? What's he gonna do, rob me for an eighth of shrooms? Kidnap me? Kill me? Then who's he gonna listen to in the afternoon?

I don't tell anyone about the deal, because smoking dust is looked down upon in my circle. Back in school, they show you the movie where the guy rips out his own eyeball off that shit. I don't know about all that, that's the same movie that said weed would kill you. I've never done dust; all I know is, it's in the same food group as ketamine and I like that shit.

I'm out of K and I don't have a connect out here in LA, so sherm might just be the answer. I snorted up my last bit a few weeks ago with my little nineteen-year-old homie. We were sitting at the dining room table passing the plate back and forth, listening to Frankie Valli.

I tell him, "I'm running outta cats to do drugs with; all my homies are going to rehab from fucking with that heroin. That shit's the devil, bruh."

He tells me, "That's funny you should say that. Don't say anything to anyone, but I've been off it for thirty days now. Once I've been clean for a year, I'll tell my sister."

"That's your business. Be careful with that boy, though." I snort a line; the dude's face goes all fun-house mirror on me. And I say, "I watched it take a gang of people out. You either end up a fucking loser or in AA, and I don't know which one is worse."

"Have you ever tried it?"

"Nah, if I tried that shit I'd be a straight junkie in no time. A man's gotta know his weaknesses and respect them." I pause for effect. "You gotta respect your weaknesses."

A couple weeks later, he OD'd. His sister found him in his room slumped over and blue, music blasting. She's in her bathrobe, titties flopping out, smacking him up, trying to wake him.

He's all right now, I guess. She's fucked-up though.

She told me not to do drugs with him anymore. Fair enough.

So here I go again on my own. Heading down to South Central to swap these things. I'm bumping Prince, singing along at the top of my lungs. It's dark when I get there. I'm in the fucking hood, the street is active. And Solo's house is pitch black.

I call him up. "I'm here. This the right address?"

He says, "You in the Black Grand Prix? I see you, come around to the alley. You good, I'm watching for you."

I get out the car, and I'm walking down the street looking for this alley. I walk up on what looks like a fenced-in road. Is that the alley? These dudes are standing there; one of them might be Solo.

It's not Solo.

It's some gangbangers posted up in a driveway selling dope. I try and play it off like I just decided to take a stroll, have a glance at the fence post next to them, and now that I've seen that fence post, I'll just be on my way.

They're staring at me like I'm crazy. I must look it, some white dude with glasses, a button-down, and hard bottoms wandering their streets looking lost. The Mexicans are mugging me; the black one in front says, "You looking for somebody?"

I'm shook, but I'm trying to hold it together. "Yeah, I'm looking for Solo."

"Well, you better call him."

"Yeah, I'm 'bout to."

I dial the phone, turn, and leave. It goes straight to voice mail. Shit. The black dude calls out, "Ay! What kind of car you driving? What size are them shoes?!"

I pretend like I don't hear him and keep walking. The phone rings. "Jude, what the fuck are you doing?"

"I'm looking for the alley. Ain't no fucking alley!"

I can feel their eyes on me.

"Just calm down, son. You in the hood."

"No shit, I'm in the hood."

I get back in the car and he tells me where I need to go. It's the alley behind his house. It looks like where Ricky got shot in *Boyz n the Hood*, but way shittier with stray cats and more trash.

He's outside waiting, a big bald dude with a mustache. He don't look nothing like Jinx. I follow him through the back of his house.

"Welcome to my crib, Angelini, it ain't that big but it's mine. We doing the best we can." It looks like your typical hood house, pit bull puppies and dirty dishes in the sink. I walk through the kids' room; they got the bunk beds and computer desk pushed up on each other with a flat-screen wedged in the corner on top of the dresser. They're watching cartoons. "Ay, y'all, meet Rude Jude, this the man we listen to on the radio when you get home from school." They say hello, I barely even look at them, just mumble a hi. I'm still shook from running up on them gangbangers in the dark of the night.

We go into his living room; it's cramped. He's got an armchair with a TV tray in front with Hennessy on top, a digital scale, and some Newport 100s. Next to it's a love seat pushed against the wall. On the other wall he's got the giant sixty-inch flat-screen from the nineties, faded picture with the big speaker underneath. The Clippers are playing. I sit in the love seat.

"Welcome, my man, welcome. This where I live, dude, shit is crazy out here. This the motherfuckin' hood, Jude."

"Yeah, man, I could tell. I met your neighbors."

"Jude, them boys are wild, but they good wit me. They my

lil killers if I need something." He pulls out a cigarette but doesn't light it. He's shaking his head. "Boy, this shit out here, my nig? It's like another world. Look at this shit right here; this shit happened just this morning in my backyard. This my house, dude."

He's pointing to the computer screen on the other side of the armchair. It has six tiny boxes, surveillance from all over the house. He's clicking shit with his mouse.

The screen shows his backyard with four cholos standing there; they're just chilling. Three circle the one in the red shirt; you see him tense up. They rush him, they're punching him in the head, he bangs into the fence, he falls down. They're on him, he scrambles to his feet. They're swinging wild catching him in his face, he's fighting back, blood's pouring out his nose.

Solo lights his cig. "This eleven today, dog, in the morning, look at this shit! This the Forty-Second Street Gang, so he gotta get busted in his head forty-two times before it's over."

"How do they know when they're done?"

"You can't see it but there's a bitch in the corner with a clicker counting. . . . Oooh look at him, he's leaking!"

It's going on forever; it feels like he got hit way more than forty-two times. I'm thinking, good thing he don't live on Ninety-Eighth Street. Shit, good thing I don't live down here. I know I'm not tough, but this is just a reminder of how soft I really am. I just want him to turn this shit off.

Solo's face is in the screen, "Hold up, hold up. I wanna see the bald-headed cat get knocked!!"

Red Shirt's bleeding everywhere, but he's still fighting back. Baldy swings, loses his footing, and runs his jaw dead into Red Shirt's right hook. His head snaps back, his body goes limp, he crumbles. They stop fighting, the other two drag Baldy away. An OG walks in from offscreen with a chick. She hands him a towel to clean up and gives him a hug.

I say, "He's got heart."

Solo takes a drag off his Newport. "He's in the gang now."

I nod. "He's in the gang all right."

Solo pulls out a tiny vial filled with gold liquid and hands it to me. "Here you go, Jude, Gorilla Piss, formaldehyde. Open it, smell that shit. Stink right?"

I do, it does.

"What you gonna do is, you dip a cigarette in that shit, let it leak all the way up, then you smoke that shit. Just make sure you in a comfortable environment around some people you trust cuz this sherm boy . . . I'm telling you."

"I'll prolly just do it with a chick and fuck."

"That's cool, this shit'll make you wanna beat the breaks off the pussy. Just don't even tell her it's on the cigarette, let her hit it first. Then you hit it. Get her fucked-up. It'll be like a surprise."

I look at him like he's crazy. "I ain't gonna surprise no girl with sherm, have her bugging out in my crib, breaking shit."

"Whatever, do what you wanna do. But this shit turns you straight gorilla! And just be around some good people that ain't gon' judge you cuz you might end up buck naked."

"Solo, you be doing this shit?"

"Me? Nah, not in like ten years since I had my youngins. I had to go to rehab off this shit, so be careful."

I get up to leave, I tell him about the mushrooms, tell him to go hit a park about a half hour away, get with nature. He looks at me like I'm nuts. "Man, I ain't going to no woods! I'm finna stay right here in the hood and trip out. Soak 'em in cognac and bug out off the floor, like I'm in a boat."

I give Solo a pound and a bear hug, then get in my car and drive off. I sing along with Prince, but it comes out a whisper.

I'm thinking about who I can do my drugs with. All the chicks I'm fucking with right now are in AA. And none of my homeboys are dumb enough to do it with me. So the sherm's still sitting where I put it when I got home, in my refrigerator door, right next to the mustard.

robocop

I'M SPREAD-EAGLE ON THE CHEROKEE, PALMS on the roof. They're running through my pockets throwing their hands up my ass crack, on my balls. Asking where we been, where we're going. Dont's next to me, answering questions. Jinx and Myron are on the other side of the Jeep getting the same treatment.

We're trying to go to Canada but we can't even get out of Pontiac. Getting fucked with by the police is nothing new. We've spent many a night sitting on the curb watching the cops rifle through our shit; tearing up our cars. Bust our chops over a blunt-roach or weed stem, then let us go. Sometimes they even plant something on ya—did Jinx like that when he was out with a chick. Put a twenty-dollar rock on his seat, then arrested him. Court ordered him to attend NA meetings.

They don't find anything. We're clean. We're telling these guys the truth. We're trying to go gig in Canada. Me and Dont aren't old enough to get into half the bars out here and you only gotta be like nineteen to drink there. They fuck with us a little while longer then let us go.

It's then we decide that maybe I should drive, cuz I'm white and the cops'll be less likely to fuck with us if a white guy's driving. So we're speeding down I-75 trying to get to Windsor before the bars close. And the whole time they're talking shit about what a lousy driver I am.

It's the truth. I'm the worst. My old man tried to teach me stick on his Chevette, but I kept stalling out, running up on curbs. And he'd be in the passenger seat, freaking out, screaming on me. For good reason: that Chevette was the only car he had and he couldn't afford for me to wreck it. So he stopped with the lessons and I just waited till I turned eighteen, took the written test, and got a license.

I kind of learned how to drive from video games. I thought the more I swerve in and outta traffic and the faster I go—the better I am at driving. So we're gunning it down the freeway, Big Mike banging in the stereo, Jinx riding shotgun and he's leaning out the window trying to holler at a carload of girls driving next to us.

They speed off. I chase 'em. We're going ninety. They exit on Mack and I keep driving. It's a quarter past one and we gotta make it to the club before they close.

Ninety on the freeway isn't that fast. But it is fast when the highway goes from 70 to 35, due to a sharp curve to the right that dumps you off on Jefferson. That's just what this freeway does, and I didn't see this, cuz I'm busy trying to chase women and impress my friends.

Dont and Myron see it first and they're yelling, "Jude, Jude! Watch the turn!"

I look back at 'em, then look at the road and I'm at the turn before I even know it. I get it down to sixty but we're still skidding off the freeway. They're hollering in the backseat. Big Mike's still banging. I look at Jinx. He shakes his head, says, "Smash." I cut the wheel back toward the median and we flip.

I leave my body for a second. I'm hovering over my shoulder watching it happen, watching us roll and roll. Then it feels like I got hit in the head with a cinder block. Then it goes black.

It's peaceful.

I wake up to Dont smacking me on my face; my head's dangling out the driver-side window. "Jude, wake up, man! Jude! Wake up!"

I come to. He opens up the door. I stagger out, blood leaking out of my head. I collapse on the side of the road. His Cherokee's back on all four tires but it's demolished—roof caved in, speaker box coming out the back, all the windows shattered.

I say, "Shit, Dont, I'm sorry about your car, man. I'm so sorry."

"Don't even worry about it. You good?"

"I'm straight. How I look?"

My pants and shirt's all ripped up. I got all types of blood coming out of me. He says, "You look good, cuz, you look good."

"Is everybody else good?"

"Yeah, we okay."

"Shit, where's my pager?" I look down at my legs. "Man, I fucked up my Hilfigers!" I look up and see Myron's got three girls who must've walked down from the projects tending to his wounds. "Where my fuckin' girls at? Tell one of them bitches to come over here!"

When the ambulance comes they take me to Detroit Receiving. I sit in the holding room for hours, waiting for an X-ray. They said I might've broke my neck. I'm next to a bum who smells like liquor and piss and week-old dick. He keeps yelling for his catheter to be changed. Across from me is a black kid with a gunshot wound, handcuffed to a gurney. He don't say nothing.

Jinx, Myron, and Dont are bedside talking shit.

"Jude, you sposed to drive on the wheels of the car. Not on top of that bitch!"

"I'm sayin'! You can't drive for shit! You the fuckin' pits, dog!"

"Ay for real! Get better and all that, but I swear to God, nigga, I ain't even getting on a skateboard witcho ass!"

We're laughing but I'm trying not to laugh too hard, cuz I'm afraid I might break my neck some more.

My dad shows up, he's got a disposable camera from Kmart. He's all upset. He's in my grill taking pictures.

I tell him, "Get that shit out my fuckin' face."

"Fuck that, you're gonna remember this, what you did to yaself!" And he's back in my face snapping.

X-rays come back. I got a hangman's fracture; C-2 and C-3

vertebrae are cracked. Doc says it's one of those "Supposed to die" injuries. Said I was a cunt hair away from being dead or crippled, pissing myself, driving around in a wheelchair using a straw.

They give me the Halo-Vest. I'm halfway sedated when they do it. I can feel them shaving my head. I can feel the razor going over the open wounds, catching the glass embedded in my skull and pulling it out. Every stroke I can feel it. There's a lot of glass. I can feel them screwing the posts into my skull, in my forehead and behind my temples. It feels like my head's in a vise and they keep tightening it. I'm writhing and moaning.

I hear the sweet words of a nurse telling me, "It's okay, honey, it's gonna be okay." And she's stroking my hand.

I go home the next day. I'm staying at my grandparents'. People come to see me the first week, I get a lot of visitors. After a while, it dwindles. I'm not mad. That's what happens when you get sick or go to jail. People care about you, but life goes on, they gotta live it. You don't fit in theirs anymore.

Chicks I was fucking cut me off and my homeboys disappeared.

A month in I'm so bored, I'm going crazy. All I do is listen to books on tape and old radio shows from the forties: *Fibber McGee and Molly*, that kind of shit. I start trying to seduce my nurse, I try to get her to wash my dick in the shower. She does once, which is cool except for the fact she's a forty-five-year-old, 250-pound black lady. It's more like getting my dick washed by Tyler Perry than anything else.

I just need to get out the house. I need to be somewhere,

anywhere that's not the doctor's office or my grandma's. So I start bugging my dad to take me to go see *Batman and Robin* when it comes out. It's kind of a big deal. This is back in the day before every goddamn week they dropped a comic book movie. This shit would happen like once a year, maybe.

I'm like, "Pop, we gotta go hit that new *Batman* when it comes out."

He looks at me. "Whataya fuckin' crazy? Ya neck's broke. What if we're out there and ya get hit and ya can't use your legs anymore?"

"Man, ain't nobody gonna hit me!"

"Look atcha. You got all of this shit comin' outta ya head. Ya look like fuckin' Robocop. Someone could hit ya on accident and bam! Ya crippled."

"Pop, I'm good! Nothing bad's gonna happen. I just wanna see George Clooney, man."

"You never even watched *ER*; you don't like Clooney! I'm not taking ya. If we drive there and get in a wreck, ya dead! I'm not taking ya, that's it. Okay Robocop?"

I stayed on him for two weeks till he folded. Opening night, me, him, and Rachel, we drove crosstown all the way to the Star Theater in Rochester to see it. We left an hour and a half early just so we could be the first people in line, so we could sit in the handicap seats. The whole drive over, it's like driving through a minefield. Every car that passes us—he's cussing at 'em; every intersection—he's freaking out, looking for stray cars that might be running red lights, that might run into us. He just doesn't want me to die. Rachel and I could give a shit.

We're the first ones there. First in line. Eating our popcorn, feeling good. I'm out, baby, I'm out.

Pop's still stressed. "Look, when they take the tickets, walk as fast as you can and grab the handicaps. Okay? I don't want anybody fucking bumpin' ya, makin' ya worse."

"Okay."

"Rachel?"

"Okay."

Some teenager takes our tickets and my pop goes flying to the theater in a forced march; Rachel and I are trying to keep up. Some nerds are trying to race us, but we're whooping them. We beat everybody to the theater. We're the first ones there. We get in and sure enough, there's a couple sitting smack dab in the middle of the retard seats eating candy, waiting for the movie to start.

Pop damn near loses it.

"What the fuck is this?" He runs up on 'em. He's standing over 'em. "Excuse me . . . my kid, he broke his neck and he's got this shit on his head, I don't want him to get bumped, so could ya move over a couple seats?"

They just look up at him.

"Could ya please move over for my kid. He's got a broken neck."

Nothing.

He explodes. "Look, mothafucka, my kid needs to sit in the fuckin' handicap seats so would you fucking move?!"

Hard cases. They still won't move.

The theater's filling up. There aren't as many places to sit.

Now people are watching him. I see the mother of a girl I went to school with and a librarian I used to work with staring at my dad. I smile, wave to them, and go help my dad. I stand over the couple. With a cage screwed into my head. Everyone's watching. I say, "Fuck these motherfuckers! Whoop their ass, Pop! I'll smack the shit out this bitch! Get the fuck out these seats!"

Pop jumps in. "Let my fuckin' kid sit here!"

"Yeah, bitch! Let me sit here!"

Just then, some guy in the audience yells, "Hey, buddy, they're deaf!"

Sure enough, we look down and these motherfuckers are scared as hell signing to each other.

Pop's says, "What the fuck are deaf people doing at the movies?!"

I'm like, "I guess they read lips."

"They didn't read our lips."

The chick looks like she's about to cry. I look down to her and mouth, "I'm sorry we threatened to beat you up. I thought you all was some assholes, not deaf." I'm using fake sign language, punching my fist to my palm and pointing at my ears.

My pop says to me, "Don't you ever fuckin' apologize for me."

Now I'm telling him I'm sorry. I try and touch him but he don't wanna be touched.

And they still won't move, so we sit right behind them and Pops stares daggers through their skulls the whole way through.

splitsville

BACK WHEN JULIE AND I BROKE up for like the fourth time, she says, "This is it, you're breaking up with me again?"

I say, "Yeah."

She's crying, she says, "You don't fight for me." She's jamming her shit into paper bags, getting her heels from under my bed, clearing out the drawers. "I can't believe this. We're breaking up like this? You have nothing to say?"

"What's there to say, Julie? We breaking up again, that's what we do. How many times we gotta do this? How'm I sposed to fight for you, when we can't stop fighting?" It sounds like a cliché the minute I say it.

She says, "You're afraid of love. You're a coward. You don't know how to be loved and you're gonna get old and be alone and no one is gonna be there to love you. You're gonna be old and alone because you're scared. And I pity you."

We stare at each other.

I tell her, "Don't forget your running shoes."

I walk her to the car and we cuss each other out some more. I tell her to put my shit outside, I'll come get it when she's at work. She says she's keeping it. She slams her door and drives off. And that's the last I see of her.

I walk back upstairs, she left a paper bag full of her shit on my bed. I leave it by the back door for a couple of days. I don't know what to do with it. I was gonna throw it out but Andrea tells me not to. So I shove it in my closet and I pretend like it's not there.

captain caveman

I COME HOME TO MY MOTHER on the porch, smoking a cigarette, crying. She only smokes when she's upset. She thinks I'm shooting up ketamine; she saw the vial sitting on the night-stand next to the bed. I hug her, I tell her I'm not.

"I put it in a pan and bake it, till it crystallizes, then I crush it up and snort it, Ma. I snort it, I don't shoot it."

We're in the kitchen and she's still crying. "I just feel bad that you get so down sometimes that you use drugs."

"Ma, I'm all right. Everybody uses drugs, everybody self-medicates. I just don't drink or smoke weed, that's all. I tried drinkin' but it made me depressed. I'm not even snortin' K right now. I got that shit for LA, when I go back. Right now I'm on Vicodin and you fuckin' up my high."

I smile. I'm trying to make her laugh. She doesn't.

"I just don't like needles."

"I'm not using no needles. I'm not Ronnie. I'm not dumb."

Ronnie's her ex-boyfriend. He's this hood cat from Seven

Mile, he's a couple years older than me. Used to sell dope then he started using it. He lived with her for damn near two years, leeching off her the whole time.

He'd talk to you like a crackhead, like he was running game, like he knew you—real friendly, compliment you on bullshit, then ask for favors.

He'd be like, "I like them shoes, Jude, where you get 'em? I'ma buy me some, them shits is sharp. I know you got the hookup wit Eminem, get me some Rocawear, Jude, get me some Fubu. What's up on your girlfriend? She Colombian, right? She got the coke hookup? She got that yola? Let's make some money. We need to hit the club, go gig, man. I'ma come out to New York and chill witchoo, man. You can take me to Harlem." And so on. Like we was best friends.

I'd space out; my eyes would glaze over and I'd just tell him, "Naw, man, nah."

I'd look at my mom like, why do I gotta deal with this fucking asshole when I'm in town? Why's he living around your teenage daughter?

That's how she's always been, trying to save somebody, save yourself. I used to say if you wanna fuck my mom all you gotta be is homeless at the bus stop; she'll find ya. And Ronnie'd be in the kitchen cooking up food that my mom bought, acting like he was doing her a favor, talking 'bout, "I can burn, man! I can burn. Whatchoo know about that, Jude?"

And I'd tell him, "Nothing."

Rachel hated him; I didn't. You can't get mad at a junkie for being a junkie; they are what they are. It's like getting mad at the sky for being blue. What the fuck did I care who my mom messed with? It's her life.

When she moved out to Cali, we thought she was done with him but he followed her out on the Greyhound. I'm on vacation with Julie, wine tasting, and I'm getting phone calls from my mom asking do I have OxyContin hookups in San Francisco. Ronnie's outta methadone and having withdrawals.

I had hookups, but I tell her, "Nah."

I'll let a junkie be a junkie, but I'm not saving a junkie. Fuck him.

She left Cali a few months later, Ronnie stayed, and that was that.

I get why she's in the kitchen now crying over her drug-using son and how she feels guilty for it. She blames my childhood. I never blamed the drugs on that. I'd prolly have the same vices, happy childhood or not.

I put my arm around her and we go out on the porch to play cribbage and I sneak a Dilaudid and try not to nod off during our hand.

She wins.

I joke about it a couple nights later, how my ma was tripping thinking I was shooting up ketamine, and nobody laughs. They're concerned, too. I'm the only one that knows I'ma be all right. I'm just going through a tough time right now, that's all.

I fly back to Cali, back home. Alone. I'm sniffing these drugs watching foreign cinema, missing my family already. I don't do well by myself. I need people. It's how I process things, I bounce it off of 'em. If I got no one to talk to, these thoughts just bounce around in my head. I obsess. So I take something or fuck something just to leave my brain for a bit.

I'm sitting on the couch and I'm tired. I'm tired of it all, the going out, the drugs, the fucking, LA, everything. I'm tired of trying to meet new girls. These chicks out here got messed-up values and an inflated sense of self-worth.

They grew up getting trophies for finishing fifth. Their parents told them they're special when they're not. They're average at best. You gotta work at special and most people don't.

And that's what's awaiting me out there in public. A bunch of average motherfuckers who think they're about some shit, not returning my phone calls.

I'm watching this world pass me by. I don't know if I wanna catch up, cuz I'm not sure I like where it's going. I'm the last of a generation, I'm a troglodyte snorting K on the couch. I'm a goner. I'm bitter. I'm jealous.

Kev hits me to go to dinner. I leave my pity party and meet him in Silver Lake. We're in the thick of it. Youth in revolt; they're bucking the system and paying for it with their parents' credit cards.

We're talking, catching up, and this douche bag's behind me in my ear blabbing about himself to his date. The motherfucker's twenty-five years old talking about all the crazy shit he did in high school. This motherfucker's claimin' high school. "And then I used to make pipe bombs outta cherry bombs and Mountain Dew bottles and I was into graffiti. . . ."

I look back and she's nodding like she's interested. Jesus

Christ. I hope they don't reproduce. I take a bite of noodles and block him out.

It's time to pay. I put half on it. It's cash only and Kev's gotta hit the ATM up front. Someone else was there, the douche bag's date. They're going Dutch.

We're outside. I'm like, "Hell naw. That bitch had to pay to listen to that lame talk? Fucking idiots deserve each other."

I'm seeing it all the time, these chicks out here with lames going Dutch thinking they're being progressive. What the fuck is Dutch? We ain't in Holland. They come out, hop in his Prius with the Obama bumper sticker, and drive off to Echo Park. I laugh. Figures. I hope they crash along the way.

Kev's homies hit us to go to La Poubelle for a drink but we seen enough for the night. Kev heads home for video games and weed; my homegirl meets me at the crib for choke-out sex.

I beat it up good, I wring her neck. She likes it. I needed it, too. I hadn't had good sex in a minute. I cum hard and collapse on the bed. I'm lying there trying to catch my breath.

She says she's thirsty, asks do I want her to get us some water. I tell her, "Naw, girl, chill there. I got you."

I get up and go get her some water. Cuz she's a guest in my house. And I'm a fucking gentleman.

this is sparta

I'M AT A DINNER WITH FRIENDS and this writer's talking shit about some other writer. He keeps saying her writing's lazy, and the table's quiet so he says it again and again. No one listens, they just wait for their turn to talk. I'm just waiting for him to stop. I pick at my food.

He's been at it for a while, this gay blue-blood. He's got the AIDS face, cheeks sunk in with the bones popping out. I'm not saying he's got it, but I'm not saying he doesn't. Either way, I don't give a shit, I'll share a plate with him. Fuck it.

Now he's talking about what's the best month to get a good lobster, because they molt and they get skinny when they molt and you shouldn't buy one then. But he doesn't know the month. I try to be social, chime in about crustaceans, but the writer ignores me and another one talks over me, talking about where to go to eat good pizza. Now AIDS Face is on about taco stands and tamales in Boyle Heights.

Fuck these dudes. I focus on the redbone across from me with her cleavage out. She might not have the emotional depth that I'm looking for in a woman, but at least her tits are jiggly and she's nice. I pour her tea and she starts talking about running trains.

She's slurping her soup, talking 'bout some dude she's fucking with, how he's texting her trying to get her to run trains.

I ask, "How old is he?"

She says, "Twenty-five, and he's crashing on his sister's couch."

"Little old to be claimin' trains. Little old to be staying on the couch."

She tells me he's broke because he works at a nonprofit.

"No shit."

I pour her some more tea and decide I'm good on her. Copping pleas for a deadbeat that's trying to run trains on you—that shit's disheartening.

We used to do it in our formative years back at Countryside. But we ain't call 'em trains, we called 'em bustos. Get a thirteen-year-old, bring her to the crib, and everybody fucks her while Donte goes through her purse.

I think about that sometimes, the chicks we used to fuck all grown-up now, probably somebody's wife, somebody's mom. Think about how they used to get tossed up and fucked by the crew.

It kind of hurts my heart.

I hope my mom didn't get tossed up. Who knows; it was the seventies. I guess that's why they say the past is the past. Probably somebody with a whore girlfriend came up with that one. Ya can't help who you love.

The chick's still going on about her fucking dude. I'm barely listening, eating soup, stealing looks at her tits. Yeah, I'm good on this one. I don't need another dumb redbone, I got one of my own.

Mine, she comes by the studio and sucks my dick whenever she's mad at her boyfriend.

I'm like, "Hey, blah blah blah, how you doing?"

Then she tells me how her mom's running up her cell phone bill and fucking up her credit. And how her man's dogging her, how he won't eat the pussy. I've smelled her pussy; I don't blame him. I nod and give her advice, then after a while I get up, walk to her, stand above her, and place her hand on my crotch.

Then she rubs it and says, "What are you doing?"

It's the dance we do.

I take my dick out and put it in her mouth. She starts slow like she doesn't want to, then she picks up the pace. She sucks me till I cum and swallows. Then I go back to my chair, carry on with my radio show, and wait for her to leave.

One time after she finished she says, "Jesus Christ. Why do I come here? I can't believe this, what do you do to me, Jude? I don't even let my boyfriend cum in my mouth."

I look at her. I say, "Maybe you should."

Her man ended up inheriting a hundred thousand bucks and dumping her ass.

We have a falling-out cuz I still won't fuck her. I tell her, "If you're acting this crazy over sucking my dick, how you gonna act if I fuck you?"

She's calling me pieces of shit via text. I wanna tell her if she'd just smarten up, get some sense, maybe wash her pussy a bit, she might be a decent catch. But I don't.

She showed up at my job the other day. I was half tempted to put my dick in her mouth while her girl waited outside. Mind-fuck her, tell her she could suck but she wasn't allowed to swallow—nut in my hand and wash it off in the sink.

Teach her a lesson, kick the dog.

Dealing with this broad brings out my sadistic side. I feel like I'm seven again, plucking the legs off a spider, watching it writhe. I understand bullies; they see something weak and they want to destroy it.

Spartans, when their kid came out retarded, they just chucked 'em off the mountain. Now we raise them. And I hear the parents say how lucky they are to have 'em in their life. But when I see 'em at McDonald's, with their kid drooling all over the place, hitting the normal one with his slimy little hand, the parents don't look lucky; they just look tired.

I was at the studio, and looking at her mouth, thinking of what to do with it. I wanted to break her little brain. But I kept my dick in my pants and told her it's through. End of the line, no more head.

She left.

Now I'm at dinner, listening to AIDS Face prattle on about the last book he wrote and why it's not published, when she texts me again to see if I really meant it. I don't hit her back. I take a sip of my tea and swallow.

board games

I WAKE UP IN A FOUL mood. The weekends are the hardest for me; they always have been. One has to find things to do to fill all that time.

In New York, I'd get hookers, day shift. I didn't have any friends there, just chicks I was about to fuck or done fucking. First time I got one, I had to take two trains down to Chinatown. I meet up with a Chinese pimp on the corner. He's wearing a wifebeater, dress pants, and flip-flops, smoking a cigarette, digging in his nose with his pinky.

I follow him into a railroad apartment, down the hallway, past three old whores watching a black-and-white TV, squatting around a Crock-Pot, bubbling. It smells like ginger and onions.

I'm in a room with a kiddie bed covered with paper towels; on the nightstand is a roll of toilet paper, lube, and some rubbing alcohol. Mine comes in wearing a baby-doll dress, she looks about fifty, no English.

She gets the lube, squirts it in her hand, applies it to her crotch, and bends over. I take her like that and try and get it over with quick. She cleans me with the rubbing alcohol. I leave tingling and get a slice of pizza.

That used to be my weekend. I broke that habit a few years ago. Every time I wanted an escort, I'd buy a backgammon set instead, take it to the cigar shop, and play. I got ten of 'em.

Guys would be like, "That's a beautiful board, how much that one cost ya?"

I'd tell 'em, "One and a half hookers."

They'd get a good laugh out of it, then go back home to their wives.

It's ten in the morning. I'm in the market for a credenza, so I go antiquing, then I hit a movie. I make plans with Annie to snort these drugs and fuck. I got a few hours to get my mind right. She's late, what do I care? Not my girl. We snort till it burns, till I see pink wolves. We fuck for hours, till the drugs wear off and I'm tired of her and she goes home.

She leaves and I'm on Craigslist looking for prostitutes, phone in one hand, dick in the other, pressing numbers. I don't call the hooker. I just jerk off to her picture, go throw up in the toilet, and go to bed. I dream of Julie that night and the night after.

I wake up at six begging for it to stop. It's been over a year and a half and I still see her, I still miss her. I know her number by heart. I wish I could just forget it.

We haven't spoke since the split. I broke down and called her this afternoon. I needed to know if she was over me cuz I'm not over her. What should we do about it? I'll come crawling back, just let me. Just answer the phone. I leave a message.

I been staring at my phone all day waiting for it to ring. Maybe she's busy, maybe she's working. I drive by her work. She's not there. I try her again. No answer, no message, I don't even know what to say. I text her.

Nothing.

Maybe I'll hear from her when I'm stronger.

jude the dude

THIS MARRIED CHICK HITS ME UP on Facebook talking about wanting phone sex. I email her, "I ain't picking up the phone till I get some nudes sent my way."

She writes, "Nudes? I can't send you naked pictures, that's like cheating."

"What the fuck you think phone sex is?"

She sends me a headless bra-and-panty shot with her phone number. She's got some big-ass titties.

A few days go by, I'm at some art school dance party in Bushwick, lots of drugs, lots of ironic mustaches. I'm gone off Norcos and ketamine. I don't know why I mix the two together; they seem to cancel each other out. But I keep on snorting and popping pills. I hit on this chick in front of her man. Not being disrespectful, I just thought he was gay.

He says, "Hey, man, that's my girl."

I pat him on the back. "Oh, for real? My bad, I thought you sucked dick."

I go outside. I'm feeling kinda grimy. I walk down the sidewalk, past the art fags and hip-hop dykes. Lemme call this married bitch, tell her what I want her to do with my dick, let her catch a nut. I dial her number. It rings and rings. Her voice mail comes on. Fuck it, dumb idea anyway. I don't leave a message. I go back inside and dance around to synth-pop.

A week later, she emails me, says her husband saw our messages. She keeps hitting me up about giving me head. I ignore her. This lady's crazy.

I get an email from some guy. I open it.

Hey scumbag, have fun letting my wife suck your dick, she's real good at it.

I just went through this a few months back, getting pranked by some computer tech whose girl tried to holler at me. He had a program that did it for him, called me every twenty minutes and left a message. At the end of the day he calls me, talking through a voice-distortion box, sounding like Darth Vader and shit.

"HEY ASSHOLE, HOW'D YOU LIKE ALL THE PHONE CALLS?"

"Is this Jen's dude? Why are you playin' on my phone?"

"HAHAHAHA."

"This is so fucking lame, dude. She told me she was single."

"SHE'S NOT FUCKING SINGLE, SHE LIVES WITH ME."

"Well, I don't know what to tell you, man, she's stepping

out on you. Better talk to her. Personally, dog, I don't even know why you still messing with her."

"I KNOW. I KNOW. I SHOULD DUMP HER."

"Yeah, I hear you. You sound like a good dude, you deserve better, though."

I didn't have the heart to tell him she blew me and swallowed and probably went back home to his house and kissed him on the mouth. Shady bitch.

That blow job's costing me sixty bucks a year: I gotta pay the phone company for number blocking. I'm not going through that again with the phone-sex girl. I block her husband's email and tell her to leave me alone.

Fucking with married chicks is a headache. I tell my boy about it; he says it's bad karma, like if I bang somebody's girl, someone's gonna come bang mine.

I tell him, "Fuck that. It's not karma, it's cause and effect. Sometimes if you mess with another man's girl, you're gonna have to deal with that man."

There's no literal universal trade-off. There's no "you stole my car so your car is gonna break down" law. You do what you do and you live with it. If some shit's gonna eat you up inside then you probably shouldn't have done it.

The question is: can I live with banging some other guy's lady?

Every fucking day of my life. Her cheating, that's between them. They got the agreement not to fuck each other over.

I just don't wanna become that grimy motherfucker that these chicks come see when they need some reassurance, so they can go back to their man feeling pretty and shit. And what do I get out of it? A nut? A notch? Freedom? The freedom to sleep alone at night.

I get a bunch of emails from the phone-sex girl; she stays on me. She says they're getting a divorce; the emails were the straw that broke the camel's back. She's in town and wants to come by the studio.

Maybe you should try and work it out, you got kids.

No dice. It's over.

She wants to fuck, she wants to cum, she wants guarantees. She says she lost her family for this.

I tell her, "Come if you want. I can't guarantee you anything."

She shows up to my job in a miniskirt. She's late, she left her kids at the hotel. She sits in the rolly chair and sucks my dick during a song break. Her husband's right, she is good at it. I bend her over the console and fuck her fast and finish quick, then send her back to her kids.

She says, "I'll be here all weekend, call me."

"I'll probably be busy."

She sees herself out and I get back on the mike. She never did cum and I still sleep alone.

street meat

I'M AT THE TACO TRUCK WITH no drawers on wearing some sweatpants and a flannel shirt, looking like I just came from the VA hospital. She's all dolled up, walk of shame style. Shirt ain't tucked right, eye makeup's smeared, hair's a mess. She's telling me about *sofrito*.

Some rockabilly Mexicans are posted up on a Honda Accord listening to Morrissey, eating tacos, eyeballing us.

I look back at 'em; I'm still high. Their headlights look like diamonds.

We started off the night with some GHB, chased it with ketamine, and got to fucking. I call it KGB. I think I do it cuz it sounds cool. I like the name better than the buzz.

She's passing out, sloppy, rag-doll riding me. My ears are ringing. I'm off in my head somewhere thinking about puppy dogs and pussy trying to lose myself in the music.

She grabs the plate of K off the bedside table and sits it on my chest. I'm still in her.

"You want some more?"

I tell her, "Naw, I'm fucked-up. How you feeling?"

"I feel good. I feel like I'm floating."

"Well, float on."

She does another line and gets back to grinding.

"Feels good, right?"

"Yeah."

I don't feel nothing. I'm numb.

She wants me on top. I try but I can't. The G's got me nodding off and the K makes me feel like I'm swimming through peanut butter.

I go down on her till the high wears off, then I break out the 5-MeO-DALT. It's my go-to fuck-drug. It's like using a cheat-code on the pussy. I get it from a kid, who gets it from a kid, who gets it from some guy with a lab in China.

You get the body buzz of ecstasy without the emotional attachment. No euphoria, so no shitty comedown, and the next day you won't be on suicide watch.

I'm sitting on the edge of the bed, scooping the 5-MeO-DALT out the bag. She's on top of the covers, telling me about how her family likes dancing on the holidays because she's Puerto Rican.

Puerto Ricans are always talking about being Puerto Rican. The first time I was out with her and her girls, it was plantains and Goya all night.

She licks her finger, sticks it in the powder, and puts it in her mouth. I do the same.

"How long's this gonna take to kick in?" she asks.

"I don't know, twenty minutes, a half hour?"

"There's no way to speed it up?"

"We can snort it."

So we do that, too. Chop up lines and take it up our nose. Feels like sniffing swimming pool water. Three minutes later we're wrecked and we're going at it again. She's moaning and I'm grunting, I'm palming her ass and she comes, and we go till the playlist ends then we put on New Order and fuck some more.

Drug sex is great. The only thing better is love sex. But if you can't get that, drug sex is a nice consolation prize. It's like sorry you didn't win the new car but take this blender as a parting gift. Well, I'm 'bout to put my dick in this blender and I'm thinking the only way this could get any better is if we could just get a little more high.

I pull out this glass meth pipe I bought to smoke DMT out of so I could trip out and find myself. I never smoked the DMT because I didn't feel like finding myself. Right now I'm happy being lost.

I put a scoop of the 5-MeO powder into the pipe, put a torch to the glass bulb, watch the powder liquefy then turn to smoke. I hit it. It tastes toxic, like I'm smoking a couch cushion. I can't hold it in; I'm hacking.

I hand it to her; she lights up and traces the bulb with the flame, evenly. It looks like she knows her way around a meth pipe. This gives me pause. She puts the stem in her mouth, takes a monster pull, and blows out a cloud of smoke.

She hands it back to me. "There's more in there, if you want it."

I look at the boat picture on my wall. The water's moving. My hands are shaking, my mouth tastes like chemicals. It's seven thirty on a Tuesday night. We're buck naked freebasing science drugs.

I hit it again, this time like her. It's a giant load. It feels like someone rang a gong in my head, colors pop, my eyes are twitching, my stomach turns. I excuse myself, walk to the bathroom, and throw up in the toilet. I rinse my mouth out in the sink and look in the mirror. One pupil's pinned, the other's the size of a nickel. I'm unshaven; I got bags under my eyes. I'm getting old.

I throw water on my face, go back in the room, and fuck her some more. We go forever and no matter what position or hole I hit, it's never enough. No matter how deep I dig in her, it's never deep enough. If I could just push my whole body inside of her I would, just to feel something more.

I finally cum and we're all fucked out. Sticky and exhausted. She's laying next to me smoking an e-cig.

"You know, you haven't been to my job yet; you should come by this week and meet all the girls. So they can see who I've been talking about."

"This week is nuts for me and next week I'm out of town."

We've been meeting like this for months, casual. I don't need to meet her friends. But I don't even wanna have that talk with her. I'm too high to have that talk.

So we get tacos instead and she's giving me the recipe to *sofrito* and I'm watching the La Bamba Mexicans finish eating their food and throw their trash on the ground. In their own neighborhood, fucking animals.

I get to thinking about my own bedroom with the covers ripped off the bed, the drugs everywhere and used condoms all over the floor.

I'm thinking how tired I am of condoms, how you gotta stop what you're doing just to put 'em on. I'm tired of the smell, the feel, but mostly what they represent—that I'm fucking a stranger.

She's still talking but I don't hear her. I take a bite of my taco, and I don't know if I want it anymore.

unicorns

I'M AT THE TAR PIT HAVING dinner when this badass chick walks in and posts up at the bar.

We're all checking her out. Z looks at me, whispers, "Look at her, she's beautiful, man."

Hamed says, "Go and talk to her."

"Nah, I'm good."

It looks like she's waiting for somebody. Her head pops up every time the door opens and when it isn't for her she goes back to playing on her iPhone.

Fifteen minutes go by, and she's still sitting there solo.

Hamed stays on me. "Go and talk to her, bro. Just say, 'Hi, my name is Jude, you are very beautiful woman.' And then she'll talk to you."

His English ain't the best, but I dig what he's saying.

I go take a piss and I get it in my head that if she's still there sitting by her lonesome when I get out, I'll go speak. I come out and sure enough, she's solo.

I walk over to her and say, "If you was my girl, I wouldn't have you waiting like this."

It sounds like some bullshit line, but it's true. I wouldn't make my girl wait.

She says, "Excuse me?"

"It's obvious you're waiting on someone and they're late, so why don't you let me buy you a drink and you can join our table, so you're not sitting here all alone."

She tells me she's good with her water and asks me my name.

"Jude."

"I know you."

"How?"

"eHarmony. We were supposed to go on a date, but I was in Spain and we lost touch."

"Oh yeah, you shoulda called me when you got back. Well, we can hang out now."

I give her my number, we talk a bit more, then her date shows up. I dip.

This dude. Fucking Hollywood cliché. He's five seven and dressed like a tool—flaps on the back of his jeans and an overworked button-down.

Hamed says, "What did you say, bro? How did it go?"

"It went well and if she don't hit me, then she's into douchey agent types and ain't shit I can do about that, now is it?"

When I left that night she hit me.

It was kismet. We weren't even supposed to hit the Tar Pit that night. I wanted burgers. Z talked me into going there, and

I see her all pretty and lonely sitting at the bar playing on her phone. If her date would've showed up on time, I never would've hollered at her, but he didn't and I did and we reconnected after linking on the Internet the year before.

It was like one of those romance movies where the rich guy's cruising the streets in his Lotus, looking for hookers and he finds a white one with all her teeth and he buys her some new clothes and dusts her off and then he sees her as the pretty woman she is and not as the whore she's acting like and they get married and live happily ever after.

I fucking love romance movies. They give me hope. Deep down, I don't believe any of it, but I want to. I want to believe in that shit the same way I want to believe in wizards and unicorns.

What I really think happens is you find a girl, get married, get divorced, and pray she doesn't rape you for half your shit. That's all I know.

But that's not all I wanna know. I wanna learn something different. Maybe some lady will pick me up, dust me off, and see me for the man I am and not the whore I've been acting like. So I was stoked when I met that chick in some serendipitous, what-are-the-odds type fashion.

I hit her to hang out that weekend.

Nothing.

Maybe I'm being too desperate, calling her when I say I'm gonna.

I let it breathe three weeks, hit her again.

This time with the text bullshit. I fucking hate texting. It's soulless.

I text her anyway, let's get up.

We make tentative plans.

I'm looking sharp.

She blows me off. No call. No show.

Fuck her.

She hits me the next day with excuses.

Whatever, it's cool.

I saw the dude she went on a date with.

She was at the bar waiting a half hour on a midget in distressed jeans and embroidered shirt and you gonna blow me off!?

So much for kismet. Sometimes coincidences are just that. Life is life and movies are movies.

And these romance movies are about as bad for my head as porno flicks. I got as much chance of Pretty in Pinking my way into getting a girlfriend as I do of performing *bukkake* on a Japanese schoolgirl.

I'm gonna find a woman I'm crazy about and that I gel with and get along with and all that shit, but I know this— when I do find her, some days she's gonna get on my fucking nerves and some days she won't and it's gonna be some work and they don't show that in the romance movies.

Now if you'll excuse me, I'm gonna go look at some porn.

gingerbread man

VAUGHN'S IN THE CAR WITH RACHEL when they pick me up at LAX. Vaughn heard me talking about PCP on the air and wants to get dusted. Rachel wants to go to a dance party. I been dancing all week in New York. The last thing I want to do is hit some fucking art-fag dance party with a bunch of youngsters downtown.

I say I'll think about both, but I'm lying about one.

Rachel hits the party. I end up getting sushi with Vaughn and Alex. We let the chef choose what we eat. I eat the face off a shrimp—deep-fried, headfirst, let's go. I offer a shrimp face to Vaughn, he don't wanna do it.

He's like, "I'll smoke some sherm but I don't know about the shrimp heads. Their legs are freaking me out."

I'm like, "Just eat that shit face-first, like you're a motherfucking monster. Merk that shit."

He goes in. I'm mashing some eel. Chasing it with green tea and Advil; my tooth is killing me.

After sushi we stop at this art show. I run across the street to holler at my boy who works the door at some trendy bar. I go there mainly to chop it up with him, but also to feel superior to these fucking hipsters on line vying to get in. When I'm running back across, I fart and shit myself midstride.

I don't even know it. I'm in the art gallery talking to some dude that recognizes me from *Jenny Jones* when I feel something wet running down my ass cheek. The bathroom opens and I clean myself up, stuff my boxers in the trash, and rage on. Whatever, I'm falling apart.

We decide we're gonna smoke the PCP at Alex's, and he'll watch us and make sure we're good. We're driving down the street banging "Born in the USA."

Vaughn's hyped; he keeps saying, "We getting dusted."

I'm driving on Hollywood looking for a head shop, with Alex's shih tzu on my lap; I'm looking for some herbal cigarettes to smoke.

Vaughn's like, "Dude, I don't get how you're gonna smoke some fucking PCP, but you're worried about smoking cigarettes."

We find a parking spot right in front of the smoke shop. Some white dude with a cholo accent helps us out; he's throwing us deals cuz he loves the dog. They don't even have the herbal smokes I drove halfway across the city to get, so I cop some Newports instead and some Whip-Its and a cracker for good measure.

We're back at Alex's getting ready. The sherm I got from Solo is in a vial inside of a prescription pill bottle. Vaughn cracks it open and it makes the room smell like a morgue.

He's like, "I don't know, man. I might like myself too much to smoke this shit. It smells like the inside of a dead body."

Alex is trying to figure out how to work some expensive camera. He thinks it'll be good for Vaughn's rap career to document this. It probably will be. These new rappers play at being crazy. We don't pretend. We eat shrimp heads and smoke sherm.

I dip my Newport in the vial and watch the liquid seep up the paper. Alex is hitting me with a light monitor. I'm blowing on the cigarette, trying to dry it.

I'm nervous. I'm pacing. I'm clowning his tiny sweater hanging up on the closet door. His housekeeper shrunk it.

He says, "Yeah, I need to put NO LAVAR signs on my wool shit to keep her from fucking it up. She keeps ruining my sweaters, but what the fuck? These are white people problems."

I'm like, "Fuck that, you worked hard to get your white people problems. Tell her to stop fucking up your shit. My housekeeper threw out two hits of my acid last month. I keep telling her not to fuck with shit in the butter drawer, but she don't listen."

Lito comes by; he's Middle Eastern with gold teeth and a knife scar across his forehead. He does graffiti and Muay Thai. He's smoking spliffs with Vaughn. I'm doing Whip-Its, waiting for Alex to figure out the fucking camera.

I'm like, "Just film it with your fucking iPhone; this camera shit's taking all day."

He tells me to chill the fuck out.

I hit the nitrous and lean back; my ears go all wawawawa

on me. I see Lito sitting across from me; he hits the spliff, gold teeth smiling. I keep doing the Whip-Its till I get rotgut.

I need food. I'm in his fridge trying to get a cupcake but Alex won't give me one. He says I won't like it cuz they're all natural.

I'm like, "Bruh, I came up all natural. My folks are some hippies."

"Yeah, but it's like vegan or something."

Vegan? What do I care? That shit looks delicious. He just doesn't wanna give me one. He gives me some Paul Newman Oreos instead.

I mash like ten of 'em. Alex finally figures out the lighting.

Let's get this show on the road.

We're in the window. I put a flame to the sherm-dipped Newport, blow it out, and pass it to Vaughn. Alex is snapping pictures. I tell him don't take my picture, I'm not a rapper, I don't need photo documentation of my drug use.

Alex is complaining about the smoke. He says it smells like death and chemicals. I can't tell. I can just taste it. It tastes like shit, it tastes like you're smoking toxic chemical shit, but it's not that bad cuz there's this minty Newport finish.

I feel the effects in minutes. Me and Vaughn are amped; it feels kinda like K but way dirtier, way shittier. It's not bad, it's just different. I keep clenching my fists and flexing my chest. Ten years ago when Alex was smoking it, he said he ran through a screen door. I get it. I don't wanna break anything but I would do the fuck outta some Tae Bo right now.

Vaughn sparks up another 'Port. He dipped his cigarette too much and he's not getting a good hit.

I say, "Here, lemme see it." I put the flame to the tip and take three or four monster pulls off the ciggy and blow that shit out. Lou Reed's playing, that's my shit. "Walk on the Wild Side."

That's when I go. I don't even see it coming. I'm dancing by the window and then I'm gone.

Alex said it looked like I was trying to read the table, I was hunched over it for such a long-ass time. On my feet, bent over, with the cigarette in my hand burning. That's when they laid me down. Eyes wide open. Snap snap snap in my ear. Clap clap clap in my face. "Jude, you there? Hey, asshole, you there?" Nothing.

Sometimes tripping out is kinda like dreaming; whatever you were thinking about that day comes to you in your head. Months back, I was in a K-hole, talking to the Mid-Life Crisis on the couch and she was telling me about how her white-trash homeboy would punch his girl in the stomach a gang of times when her period was late, and I started going in and out of reality.

I'd been reading this fantasy book about an enchanted forest. I was convinced that she was one of the tree people from my book and I'm thinking, since she's a tree person made of wood can I get her pregnant? Is the kid gonna be like half a tree or something? Will we raise it in the forest, will it have roots? Am I gonna be stuck in the forest forever? I was kinda freaking out about having a tree child but then I came to and remembered that she's a human and the condom came off in her but I finished on her belly so we should be fine.

It's the same thing here, but this time, I've been rereading *Game of Thrones* and I been trying to talk to my daughter all day. It's her birthday and I keep leaving messages but we keep missing each other, it's weighing on me. So I'm on another planet with my kid and the midget from *Game of Thrones*, and I'm not such a shitty dad after all. Alex's shih tzu is laying on my chest and I'm thinking it's the Luck Dragon from *The Neverending Story*. Now we're all cruising around the universe on the *Neverending Story* dog.

I'm gone for a while, like a half hour, laid out, eyes wide open, dog on my chest, planet surfing, when the Frenchman checks my pulse.

"His blood, he's still pumping."

I jerk up. I try to talk, my tongue's swollen, it's clumsy. I say, "Did I shit or did I cum?"

They're like, "What?"

"Did I ejaculate?"

I'm worried about both because of what happened at the art show and because Solo told me I might wanna get buck naked off that sherm and the last thing I wanna do is be on a good one, playing with my dick and not knowing it.

They tell me it doesn't smell like I shit, and just like that I'm gone again. Back to my midgets and Luck Dragons.

I'm still on the floor when the Frenchman leaves. Someone turns off the lights; hours have gone by. My spit's foamy;

it's hard to swallow. Vaughn's worried. They put on my iPod, they think I might recognize something and come to. I wanna tell you I heard some Bob Seger and some INXS but I don't know, I just don't know.

Universes and scenarios keep flipping on top of each other and on top of each other over and over again. I think I'm in the bowels of a spaceship shoveling coal. The room is pulsating with a *cuuuuuhhhaaaaaaa cuuuuuuhhaaaaaaa*. I'm toiling away with the slaves in the orange glow of the ship's furnace and Gladys Knight is singing to me. I recognize it. I come back, it's 5 A.M.

The *cuuuuuhaaaaaa cuuuuhaaaaaa* is Alex snoring. Vaughn's curled up in a ball on the couch. My stomach's wrecked; my mouth tastes like formaldehyde. Moving's difficult; my head's on a swivel. My feet feel ten feet long. Somehow I make it to the bathroom.

If kctamine's a digital buzz and mushrooms are wavy, the world of sherm is that of an abused child who has been asked to draw a picture of how he's feeling. It's a fist-gripped crayon drawing of a bad man screaming. It's not good or bad, it just is.

I don't know if I need to shit or puke, so I drop trou and lean over this toilet that feels like it's as big as a swimming pool and a hundred feet away. I'm this retarded baby *T. rex*, in the dark, wobbling over the toilet bowl trying to stay up and just like a baby dinosaur I open my mouth and "Raaaaaaarrrr-rrrrrr!!"

Out comes this black crayon scribble of Paul Newman Oreos.

I keep roaring till my stomach is empty. I flush.

I'm back on the couch, diagonal, and Vaughn's looking for milk because milk is supposedly like kryptonite for PCP, and I just need this fucking thing to be over with. But there's just almond milk, to go with the vegan cupcakes. Vaughn gives me Xanax and yogurt instead. I fall out again.

When I come to at seven, I'm still tripping balls but I can walk and I can talk, kind of. I ask Alex to show me the pictures. I need to see what happened. I don't recognize myself. I look like I'm dead on the floor. Eyes wide open, lost.

I say, "Don't show those to anybody. I got a daughter."

They're driving me home in the Volvo. I'm leaning my face against the window watching normal people go to Denny's as a family. I'm helpless. Now I understand doped-up sex workers and white slavery. Right now they could take me anywhere they wanted; they could take me to the moon.

I'm thinking about what I told Brad the night before on the fire escape, after I just finished off a plate of ketamine. I said, "Brad, I don't do drugs—I all-the-way do drugs. These motherfuckers out here are doing shit to numb themselves, that's cool. Not me, sometimes I gotta stretch my mind, make my brain do karate."

"Make your brain do karate?!"

"Make my brain do karate."

And we laughed about it.

stained

I MUST'VE BEEN THREE OR FOUR at the time. I was
little. I remember that. I remember being little and dropping
my sister off at school and running errands with my mom. I remember driving in the car with her, J. Geils Band on the radio.
My angel is the centerfold. That song broke my heart. My dad
let me look at porn, I knew what a centerfold was. I remember
looking at Little Golden Books in the backseat and kicking my
feet to the time of the blinker. I remember the generic aisle in
the grocery store and the black-and-white labels.

I remember Rochester Park, the pond there, the creek, the
swings, and the monkey bars. They were metal then. My mom
took me there to play.

I was playing by them in the water when I found my duck
egg. It was laying there in the bed of the creek by a cluster of
stones. It must've rolled out of some duck's nest. I didn't know
that. I thought they just hatched them underwater.

I picked it from the creek. It was brown and bigger than a

chicken's. I ran and showed it to my mom. We drove back to Countryside. I played with my little egg the whole way. I was gonna hatch it when I got home; I told it so.

We pulled up into the parking lot, I climbed to the front seat, jumped out of the car, and ran up the sidewalk to show my dad the egg I found.

He was waiting for us to get there. He came out of the house, hollering.

He storms right past me and goes for my mom. I follow him.

He heads my mom off at the sidewalk. She backs up. He's yelling about something. I don't know what. It's violent. They're in the parking lot, he's standing over her.

I keep tugging on him. I'm like, "Look, Dad, look! Look at this egg I found!"

Nothing.

I keep pestering him. I got it in my head that if he just sees this egg and how cool it is, he won't be mad anymore. He'll stop yelling.

He shakes me off.

My mom's yelling back now, trying not to cry.

I'm scared. I'm begging for 'em please to stop fighting. His back is to me, and he's pushing her.

We're by the Dumpster now, the three of us, out in the middle of the parking lot. Now my mom's crying.

I yell, "I'm gonna count to three!! If you guys don't stop fighting, I'm gonna break my duck egg!" I hold the egg over my head and count, "One . . . two . . . three!"

It's like I'm not even there.

I slam the egg on the ground and watch the yolk splatter across the blacktop.

It's so orange against that asphalt.

There goes my egg.

And they kept on fighting till the cops came.

a brand-new you

I THINK I SMOKED TOO MUCH PCP. I wasn't concerned about OD'ing on sherm while I was doing it; intergalactic space travel is kind of the shit. I still wouldn't call it an overdose per se, more like "overdoing it." I overdid it and ended up catatonic for hours.

When I wake up on Sunday still high, I don't even trip. I just take a cab up to the Standard hotel and eat fish tacos poolside while Detroit Daniel spins techno.

When Monday comes and I'm still disoriented with no motor skills, that gives me pause. I wake up high the day after and the day after and the day after that. I'm thinking, maybe I'm not high, maybe I'm just broken.

I don't even try to drive; I can't see straight. I walk to work every day repeating my mantra, "Sharpen up. Sharpen up. Sharpen up."

But in the quiet confines of my studio, sitting by myself,

waiting to drag my ass through the next talk break, one thought goes through my head: Fried your little brain.

I still can't remember things on Thursday, I can't do math, I suck at Scrabble, I get headaches, my dick doesn't work the same, people talk to me and I get confused. I come to terms with the fact that the sherm took a piece of me. Maybe I damaged my head; maybe I'm stupid now.

Rachel asks, "Did you google that drug?"

I tell her, "It's a little late for that now. I shoulda googled that shit before I took back-to-back sherm sticks to the face."

"You should look it up."

"Fuck that."

I don't want to, the same way I used to not like taking AIDS tests after fucking with no rubber for months.

"I'll look it up," she says, and she's banging away on the computer. She's reading to herself. "Jesus Christ, Jude." She's shaking her head. "Jesus Christ . . . Jesus Christ. Do you know what that shit does to your brain?"

"Yeah, it makes you fucking retarded. Don't tell me what it did, just tell me how to fix it."

She reads some more. "I don't know, this blog says niacin. Try some B vitamins maybe? That'll detox you. It says the effects can last up to a couple of weeks."

I take niacin. I take niacin till my piss turns orange, till it looks like a toilet bowl full of orange Crush. Till I start busting orange nuts. When I cum, it looks like a Creamsicle. My boxers look like a Pollock painting.

I go to bed every night hoping I'll sleep it off. And when I wake up with my brain slow and my head still swimming, I'm like, "You fucking idiot."

I work on forgiving myself for wrecking my brain, for wrecking my dick.

Now I'm stupid. It's not so bad. I'll go with my gut more. It's making me patient. My show sucks but I'll work that job till they fire me. Maybe I'll meet a nice girl now, maybe I won't be so picky, maybe I won't give a shit if she watches reality shows and reads *Us Weekly*.

A few years back I used to talk to this little young chick Josette. I'd call her up at five in the morning high on ecstasy talking crazy and she'd just say, "Oh, Jude, what am I going to do with you?"

That's what I'm saying to myself now. "Oh Jude, what am I gonna do with you?"

I'll work hard, I'll do my exercises, I'll take my vitamins, and I'll get better, I tell myself.

I'll get better or I'll get used to it.

acknowledgments

WHEN I SELF-PUBLISHED I EDITED THIS book with one of my best friends, Andrea Grano. She's one of the few people I trust with my voice. Thanks, Andrea. Frank Ryan drew the illustrations. Kevin Beebe handled book design, cover design, typesetting, and layout on my first batch of books; not this one but he still gets a shout-out.

Danny Angelini, Ross Rowe, Toni Prieto, Greg Adkins, Rebecca Diliberto Adkins, Brian Liesegang, Tien Nguyen, and Nicholas Palos gave me notes. Cindy Chyr told me about perpetuity. Jetta and Pendarvis helped me send the book out. Rachel Angelini wrote "About the Author."

Karyn Bosnak helped get me to Simon & Schuster and held my hand through the whole process. Thank you. I was lost. Thanks to Alison Callahan and Jeremie Ruby-Strauss for giving me a shot. Thanks to Dennis Ardi, my lawyer.

Thanks to Marshall Mathers, Paul Rosenberg, and Steve Blatter for keeping me employed while I wrote this book.

Thank you to my friends and family. These stories aren't just mine, they're ours, and you let me share them. And thank you to everyone who bought this book early on. . . . You all really helped grow this book and I truly appreciate it.

Hyena Go Hard.

about the author

JUDE ANGELINI was born and raised in Pontiac, Michigan. He got his start as a guest and comic on *The Jenny Jones Show*. He now hosts his own show, *The All Out Show*, on Sirius XM Satellite Radio. His great love of music has influenced every aspect of his life, including the rhythm of his writing style. He was first inspired to write after reading Bukowski's *Notes of a Dirty Old Man*. He felt he could share his stories without being hindered by the rules of grammar.

Although he writes from his own experiences, he loves reading Elmore Leonard, science fiction, and medieval fantasy. He also loves antiquing, and a good game of backgammon.

Jude currently lives in Los Angeles.